How to Be

a Teenage

Superhero

By Erik Parrent

Copyright 2022

2

Chapter One

October 2019

Monday burned bright and hot, especially for October.

The bus pulled up to the entrance of the Saint Felix Museum of History. Barton Harper, near the back of the bus, half listened as the teacher, Mrs. Cason, outlined her expectations for her sophomore social studies class.

"We're here for the Greek artifact exhibition," she said. "But after we've toured that exhibit, you'll be free to explore to your heart's content."

Cason continued, but Barton's attention was drawn elsewhere.

"Look at her," Barton said quietly. "She practically shimmers."

Nathan Saltzman rolled his eyes.

"I'm serious," Barton continued. "It's like she walked out of a shampoo commercial."

"And who was it last week?" Nathan asked.

"Penny what's-her-face," Barton said. "But I'm serious. Courtney's the real deal."

Mrs. Cason had finished speaking, and the class had begun filing off the bus. Barton and Nathan brought up the rear of the line.

"Barton, I want you to consider that you might be – let me check my notes, here – fickle," Nathan said.

Barton looked hurt. "Nah. I'm just a romantic at heart," he said.

"Have you talked to her?" Nathan asked.

Barton paused. "Not as such," he finally conceded.

Nathan shook his head.

"The heat's getting to you," he said. "That, and your hormones."

Mrs. Cason was waiting as they stepped off the bus. She looked at Nathan, who wore one of his trademark heavy metal t-shirts, and Barton, who was wearing a t-shirt adorned with the image of one of Saint Felix's home-grown superheroes.

"We're visiting a museum, you know?" she said.

"Yeah, we know," Nathan said.

"That's why we dressed up," Barton continued.

Mrs. Cason shook her head, smiled, and waved Nathan and Barton on.

The class entered the museum. The lobby was broad, deep, and tall, with polished marble floors and soaring columns. Other patrons went about their business while Cason gathered her class around a tall woman with long braided hair.

"Hello, class," she said. "My name is Natalie. I'll be your guide today, for our exhibit, Journey to Ancient Greece."

Barton's attention was wandering again. He watched Courtney out of the corner of his eye. She was surrounded by a clutch of her friends, and they whispered to each other, and occasionally laughed, while paying respectful attention to the tour guide.

Mrs. Cason suddenly filled his view.

"Barton," she said.

He grinned, nervous and surprised. "Yes, Mrs. Cason?" he stammered.

She eyed him, suspiciously, but with a twinkle in her eyes. "This is a school trip," she said. "Make sure your attention is where it belongs."

He nodded, embarrassed. "Yes, ma'am," he said.

She nodded, and walked away.

Nathan looked at Barton. "If the teacher noticed how obvious you are, I wonder if Courtney noticed?" he asked.

Barton, blushing, shook his head. "I hope not," he said.

They followed the tour guide through the lobby and up an ornate flight of stairs. Barton did his best to focus his attention anywhere other than Courtney.

He began to pay attention to other patrons.

He saw an older couple walking hand in hand enjoying an exhibit.

He saw a woman and a pair of teenagers, each staring at a phone, oblivious to their surroundings.

And then he saw a tall man, dressed all in black.

Something about the man bothered Barton, in a way he couldn't quite articulate.

He nudged Nathan. "Check that guy out," he said quietly.

Nathan looked at the man. "What?" he said.

"I got a bad feeling," Barton said.

"It's just a dude," Nathan said, and turned back to the tour guide.

Barton looked at the man again. He wore black – so what? Black pants, a black rollneck sweater…a black leather jacket, despite the heat. And black leather gloves.

The man stood ramrod straight, with silver-gray hair swept severely back from his forehead. His jaw was accentuated by a neatly trimmed salt-and-pepper beard. His icy blue eyes seemed to take in everything, but betrayed not the slightest feeling.

Barton felt a shiver down his spine.

The class continued to the upstairs gallery that housed the Ancient Greece exhibit. Barton stuck close to Nathan and tried to listen to the tour guide, but couldn't focus.

The tall man entered the gallery. He gazed at the various cases and pedestals with the artifacts on display. Barton noticed that there were other patrons in the gallery dressed similar to the tall man.

Barton grabbed Nathan's arm and pulled him back towards the door to the gallery.

"What the hell, Barton?" Nathan asked.

"Shut up!" Barton growled. "Look around!" Barton gestured at the patrons in black. Nathan followed Barton's gestures. He opened his mouth to speak –

The people in black pulled handguns from their jackets. The tall man pointed his at the ceiling and fired. The shot was like thunder in the confined room.

"Everyone on the floor!" he shouted.

Barton pulled Nathan and ran towards the staircase. He didn't speak and couldn't think.

He and Nathan made it to the landing when they saw the old man.

The man looked like he was a thousand years old, with leathery, wrinkled skin, a long white beard, and weathered, threadbare clothing. "You," he said, looking at Barton, "might be the one. Then again, you might not. But I'm all out of time."

Barton saw the man's hand move, faster than he would have believed possible for one so old, and a flash of gold. Then he felt the hand strike his chest.

A number of things happened at once. The old man crumbled into dust before Barton's eyes. Barton screamed. Nathan screamed.

And Barton found himself transformed.

Chapter Two

Barton raised a hand. It shimmered gold. He looked up the rest of his arm and saw he was now covered in...something, a pattern of black and gold, with markings like armor but soft and supple as silk.

He glanced around. He saw his reflection in a mirror. His face was covered by a striking mask.

He looked at his hand. He closed it into a fist. He could feel energy, like nothing he'd ever felt before, electrifying his nerves.

Nathan looked at him, jaw agape, trying to find words. "Badass," he finally sputtered out.

Gun shots rang out. Barton heard screams. He looked at Nate. "Run, Nate," he said. "Get out of here!"

"No chance," Nate said.

Barton turned to the exhibit room. One of the people in black had a weapon trained on his classmates. Mrs. Cason stood in front of the students, arms out, attempting in vain to shield the entire class by herself. Fear and anger contorted her face.

Other people in black worked on individual exhibits, using various tools, trying to crack them open.

Barton heard screaming. He heard alarms ringing. He heard the approach of running footsteps, museum security, no doubt. Any moment, there would be sirens.

Any moment, they would see him.

Any moment, the killing would start.

Something deep in his mind, a voice not entirely his own, whispered, *You know what to do.*

He nodded. He did know what to do.

He looked at Nate. "Stay down!" he cried.

Barton didn't wait for an answer as he charged into the exhibit hall.

He looked around. He could see half-a-dozen of the people in black, three men, three women.

His heart raced and his mouth went suddenly dry.

What am I doing? he thought. *Am I crazy? I don't want to die!*

He reached his first target, one of the men. He clenched his fist and threw a punch. The man rocketed back and slammed into the marble floor, out cold.

This isn't so hard, thought Barton.

He turned, looking for his next target. One of the women, clear eyed and calm, raised her pistol and pointed it directly at Barton.

"AHHHHHHH!" Barton screamed even as he charged towards her.

She squeezed the trigger. The pistol went off.

The shot slammed into Barton. He hurtled back into the wall. He heard someone screaming – it was him, he was screaming – he felt like an SUV had slammed into his chest. With effort he took a breath, then a deeper one. He ran his hand over his chest.

He wasn't hurt. There was no blood, not even a scratch in his gold and black garb. How was this possible?

The leader gestured before he, the woman, and the other three still standing pointed their weapons at him.

I'll figure it out later, Barton thought.

"Fire," the man said.

Time seemed to slow down as Barton leapt to his feet. He could see the puffs of smoke from the pistols, could see the bullets in the air as they approached him. He thought, *Run.* He was on his feet and dodging the bullets in the air faster than he could think it.

He clotheslined the woman who shot him first. He was moving towards the leader when time sped up again. Barton's limbs felt like lead, but he had no time to slow down.

He looked around, and saw an artifact on a pedestal. He knocked the artifact off.

Sorry, Mrs. Cason, he thought.

He grabbed the pedestal and lifted it into the air like a baseball bat.

He swung at the leader, connecting solidly.

The man went down.

The three remaining people in black fired at the windows.

His classmates continued to scream.

The windows shattered.

Each attacker still standing gathered one of their fallen and made for the windows. A rope ladder appeared outside, and Barton could hear the sound of a helicopter.

He placed himself in front of his classmates, arms out like his teacher, doing his best to shield them from gunfire.

The attackers loudly called to unseen comrades on the helicopter. Ropes were tossed down. Their unconscious friends were quickly harnessed and hauled up. Moments later the last of them had scurried up the rope ladders.

Barton could still hear alarms and sirens. The screaming had stopped, but he could hear sobbing from his classmates. He turned and looked at them.

No one had been hurt. Behind his mask, he smiled.

Then a voice whispered in his mind, *get out*.

"Everyone freeze where you are!"

The shout came from the entrance to the exhibit. Museum security had arrived – a trio of armed guards, wearing bulletproof vests.

Uh oh, Barton thought.

Chapter Three

Barton looked at his classmates, and at Mrs. Cason. He trusted her implicitly, but he didn't fully understand what had happened to him yet. He knew she'd do anything to help him, she was that kind of teacher, but he couldn't bear the thought of putting her or his friends in danger.

So he scanned the chamber, saw a stairwell, and ran for it.

He darted down the stairs, taking them 3 and 4 at a time. He heard loud voices behind him, include Mrs. Cason calling for him to stop. He knew some of his classmates would come after him no matter what, which meant he had to find a place to hide as quickly as he could.

He emerged a couple of floors down. Thankfully, it was deserted as far as he could see. Blaring alarms, screams and cries of panic, and approaching sirens made it hard to focus. He had to find a place to hide! He looked around – there!

Barton found an office. He looked through the pebbled glass in the door and couldn't see anyone moving. He tried the knob – locked!

He said a quick prayer and gave a sharp pull on the knob – he heard a crunch as the lock broke, and then the door opened. He darted inside, and pulled the door closed behind him.

He took a deep breath, crouching by the door beneath the glass so he couldn't easily be seen.

What just happened? he thought. *Who were those people? What did they want? Is anyone hurt?*

And what happened to me?

He closed his eyes. Fear and exhilaration whirled inside him. He took a deep breath, then another, then another.

Something felt weird. He opened his eyes. He was surrounded by a golden glow. He looked at his arm – the strange garb was fading away, like fog in morning sunlight.

Then he was regular Barton again.

He sat down hard on the cool marble floor. He thought he might cry, then felt like puking for a minute or two. Then he noticed something, a weight on his chest that hadn't been there before. He reached a hand into his shirt and pulled out a roughly-carved golden medallion on a chain.

Then he heard another voice in his head. *You did well, but this is only the beginning.*

Barton wondered if he was going crazy. *Or have I just watched Star Wars too many times?*

He had to get it together. He had to find Nate and get back to his class before he aroused suspicion.

He tucked the medallion back into his shirt. Barton rose to his feet, still shaky. He quietly opened the door and peered out.

All clear.

He stepped out. No one saw him. He started moving. He came to a different stairwell. He wasn't sure if it was the one he and Nate had first ascended, but he went up it anyway.

He heard the click of shoes on marble and looked behind him. Police officers were racing up the stairs.

Barton threw up his hands. "Thank God!" he shouted. "We're safe!"

He was taken to a first-floor meeting room, where they had already crowded the rest of his class. Mrs. Cason found her way too him first. She hugged him tightly, nearly weeping with obvious relief. She spoke so fast Barton could barely make out what she was saying, but he thought the gist of it was, *where have you been I'm so glad you're safe you're in so much trouble now sit down.*

He looked around and saw Nate. He made a beeline for his friend and took a seat beside him. His classmates immediately began telling them how they were rescued from terrorist thieves by a superhero.

Someone asked where he was. "I had to use the bathroom," he said, stammering some, because he hadn't come up with a cover story yet. "Then when I got out I got lost. Then I heard shooting and just hid until the noise stopped."

Barton played it cool. He shook his head, rolled his eyes, called them out for trying to prank him. Someone finally produced a cell phone video of the incident.

Barton looked at himself, glad in flowing gold and black, and pretended he had no idea what was going on. He finally conceded to his friends that the incident was real and returned the phone to its owner.

He smiled inside. *I looked cool*, he thought. He then looked around at his friends, who only a short while ago had been in terrible danger. *I saved them*, he thought. *I made a difference.*

Soon there was museum security, and then there were police. They asked question after question, of the group as a whole, and then as individuals. The afternoon wore into evening. Pizza and soda were provided for hungry students. Finally, the tired sophomores were loaded onto their waiting bus, and allowed to leave.

Chapter Four

The bus full of weary students pulled up to their school, hours past their expected original arrival, hours past the fall of night. A small fleet of cars, SUVs, and minivans awaited them, manned by worried, anxious parents relieved beyond words to see their children safe and sound.

They were met by the principal and other staff, who cheered and clapped when the bus pulled up. The doors opened, and Mrs. Cason emerged first. She then allowed students off one at a time to be received by their families. There were smiles, there were tears, there were hugs.

Nathan's dad arrived to pick him up. His long, bushy hair was drawn into a ponytail, and he wore a heavy metal t-shirt similar to his son's. He embraced Nathan in an enormous bear hug, and they walked to their waiting vehicle.

Mrs. Cason called Barton's name. He left the bus to be met by his mom. Her eyes were red and puffy, her make-up tear streaked. She hugged Barton tightly, without a word. For a moment Barton felt her grow weak with relief, and he supported both of them. Then, she regained her strength, and she took his hand and they walked to the family minivan.

Inside the van, Barton's little sister was waiting for them. "Hey, bro," Lucy Harper said. "You OK?"

Barton patted her head. "Yeah, I think so," he said.

"Did you get shot?" she asked.

"Lucy!" their mom shouted.

"Fair question!" Lucy shouted back.

"I didn't get shot," Barton said. "Neither did anybody else. We're all OK."

"Oh," Lucy said. "That's good."

Barton thought she sounded a little disappointed.

"My brother was held hostage by terrorists," Lucy said. "Third grade's gonna be wild tomorrow."

They rolled into the driveway of their home. Mrs. Harper, Barton, and Lucy left the minivan and went inside. Lucy flopped down on the living room couch while Barton went to the kitchen and opened the refrigerator.

"I'm starving," he said to no one in particular, taking out the makings of a sandwich and then assembling it.

He sat at the kitchen table, joined by his mother. In the light of the kitchen Barton could tell even better that the day had taken a toll on her. For a moment, she didn't speak, and merely placed her hand on his shoulder.

"I was so scared," she finally said. "If anything ever happened to you or Lucy..."

Her voice trailed off.

Barton felt guilty. He hadn't asked for whatever had happened to him that day, but it had kept him safe and alive.

He opened his mouth to speak.

What was he going to say?

A crazy old man slapped a medallion on me today?

I fought off terrorists today?

I became a superhero today?

Barton put his sandwich down, reached over to his mother, and hugged her tightly. He couldn't keep what happened a secret forever, he knew that, he *knew* it.

But he didn't understand himself yet what had really happened.

Why scare his mother before he had better answers himself?

Mrs. Harper decided that no one in their house was going to school the next day. Lucy was briefly disappointed, knowing she would miss the attendant social hubbub of the crisis, but got over it when she realized she'd get to sleep late.

Barton lay in his bed that night. He felt like every nerve was buzzing and that he'd never get to sleep.

He was asleep in moments.

He gradually became aware of the beach.

He felt the warmth first, then the smooth-rough of the sand beneath his toes. He saw that the sand was eggshell white, and then saw the crystal-clear aqua-blue of the ocean rolling up on it in gentle waves.

He turned left, and saw the beach extend a seemingly infinite distance in that direction. He turned right and saw that some distance up the beach a structure stood.

He began walking.

Soon, he was there. Barton knew he was in a dream, and that time was flowing in that way it does in a dream. But he was more aware than he was in most dreams, more in control, and he knew this was something different.

He looked around. The structure was built of white stone, bright and polished. The floors were smooth white. Columns gleamed in the sunlight. He glanced around and saw murals painted on walls, of ancient warriors and terrible monsters.

Then the old man from the museum appeared.

"Hello," the old man said.

Chapter Five

Barton almost didn't recognize him. He stood tall, and his white hair and beard were trimmed and clean. He wore a simple tunic, pants, and boots, and he was smiling.

"Who are you?" Barton asked. "Where are we? Is this...real?"

The old man smiled. "Name's Spooner," he said. "As far as I can tell, this place is...not real, exactly, but a representation. A version, of sorts, of the place the Talisman came from."

Barton reached a hand to his chest, and discovered the medallion hung there.

"The Talisman," Barton said. "That's what this is called?"

"Yes," Spooner said. "And it's what you're called now, too."

Even in this dream space, Barton felt shock. "The Talisman!" he said. "You were the Talisman?"

'I carried it, and was called by its name," Spooner said.

"You fought with Force Majestic!" Barton continued. "Back in the 1970s!"

"Yeah," Spooner said. "I was a superhero. But I fought the good fight for a long time before that…and a long time after."

Spooner gestured around them. "And we aren't the only ones. Not even close," he said.

Barton looked around. The place reminded him of what he'd learned about ancient Rome or Greece, but different somehow. Then something occurred to him.

"You're not sure what this place is, are you?" Barton asked. "You don't really know."

Spooner shrugged. "I just got here," he said.

"You didn't know before you…you know…" Barton's voice trailed off.

"Before I died?" Spooner asked.

Barton nodded.

"No, I didn't know," Spooner said. "In fact, I got the Talisman in kind of a...hurried way, myself."

Spooner looked around. "This is no place for yarn-spinning, thought," he said. Barton saw him close his eyes, and then the air swirled around them like the colors of a painting.

They now stood under a night sky, surrounded by a sea of prairie grass. A roaring fire burned close by. Barton looked closer, and saw an old, old man, with battered armor and a long, scraggly beard, lying by the fire, his head propped up by a log. Sitting on a rock, nearby, was a man dressed like a cowboy.

"Where are we?" Barton asked.

"Somewhere in New Mexico, I reckon," Spooner said. "Along about 1885 or so."

"The cowboy," Barton said, "is you."

Spooner nodded. "I was on way to meet my brother in Santa Fe," he said. "I ran across the old man by pure chance. He was burning up with fever, out of his head. I couldn't just leave him. I made camp, built a fire. I fed him, gave him some water. I hoped to get him well enough to travel, but it wasn't to be."

Barton saw the old man's hand strike out, flashing the same gold Spooner's hand had in the museum, and saw Spooner transform, his rustic look transforming into something like a Union uniform, only shimmering gold.

"I had no idea what had happened," Spooner said, as the image of the old, old man crumbled away. "I still don't know who the old man was. He never contacted me like I am you."

Spooner sat down by the fire. "But I did find out, soon enough, that the Talisman made me faster, stronger, and tougher than the ordinary man. I'm not proud of it, but for a while I didn't do much with it, other than survive, which was hard enough in those times."

Barton sat down on the other side of the fire. Spooner continued. "I discovered after a period of years that I wasn't aging right. I was staying younger than my brother, my friends, everyone around me. I started to wonder if maybe I didn't owe a debt for what I'd been given. I started trying to make a difference, any chance I could. And it became my calling."

"And now it's mine," Barton said.

"And now it's yours," Spooner echoed. "I asked the Talisman what I should do, when I felt my end coming. And it led me to you."

"Will I live as long as you?" Barton asked.

"I don't know." Spooner said. "I was only able to find out just so much about the thing in my own life. I'm a little surprised to be here, to be honest, but I figured I owed you this much."

Barton had a realization. "Are you a ghost?" he asked Spooner.

Spooner considered a moment. "I suppose I am," he replied. "But I ain't real sure what that means just yet."

"Why me?" Barton asked.

"Because you have a good heart," Spooner said. "Which don't make you perfect. Which won't save you from mistakes. But I believe the Talisman led me to you…because you'll make a difference."

32

The air grew hazy. Spooner seemed to recede, and his voice grew faint.

"I'll be in touch if I can," Spooner said, as if from a great distance.

"Fight the good fight, Barton Harper.

"Fight the good fight – Talisman."

Chapter Six

Saint Felix was not usually quiet at night, but this evening, as Barton Harper slept, was the exception. No fires lit the night. No gunfire split the silence. The wail of sirens was not to be heard.

Which is not to say that everything was peaceful.

From the outside, the townhome seemed as normal as its surroundings. On the inside, things were different.

The training room hummed with electricity. Cool air circulated and computer systems monitored the vital signs of the combatants.

One of the combatants was human.

She hadn't been able to sleep. She had tossed and turned for a good two hours before finally giving up. She dressed in workout clothes, came down the hidden stairs to the training room hidden beneath the basement level, and activated one of the drones.

The drones were roughly humanoid. They were as tall as the girl, touching six feet. Their skin was pale white, a tough ceramic laced with electronics. Where a face should be was instead a cluster of sensors that gave them a faintly insectoid appearance.

The girl sparred with the drone. Its servomotors whirred as it blocked her strikes and threw blows of its own. Its hands and feet were padded like boxing gloves, so that it wouldn't cause permanent damage.

That is, of course, if any of its punches or kicks connected with the girl, which they didn't.

She moved so fast a living observer would barely have been able to follow her. She switched between combat forms almost by the instant, from judo to kung fu to karate to krav maga, a blinding flurry of fists and feet.

The drone's combat settings had been selected to function as a normal human. After the girl had registered an attack suitable to putting a normal human down, the drone shut itself off, slumping over on its feet with a quiet sigh, the indicator lights on its faceplate going dark.

The girl frowned. She was barely breathing hard and hadn't even cracked a sweat. There were more advanced settings on the drones, but she needed her guardian's approval for those. She was loathe to wake Dagmara up in the middle of the night on one of those rare nights either of them had the chance to get some sleep.

She heard clapping.

The girl whirled around.

Dagmara sat on the stairs, smiling.

"Excellent performance against the drone," she said. "But you didn't hear me coming at all, Mallory."

Mallory Savage – Mal to everyone but Dagmara - frowned at her guardian. "I was in my own home in the middle of the night," she said, a note of irritation in her voice. "I had no reason to expect anything."

Dagmara's expression didn't change. "And this time, that expectation cost you nothing," she said. "But in the game you have chosen to play, you can and must expect anything, at all times."

"I can't keep my guard up at all times," she said. "I can't. I'm still in high school, for God's sake."

"On the contrary, high school is the best place to practice keeping up one's guard," Dagmara responded. She rose from the stairs and walked to Mal.

"I wish you'd let me drop out," Mal said. "Then I could be on the streets fighting crime full time."

"Not an option," Dagmara said. "You must have a life away from the fight. Otherwise, it chips away at your soul. I saw it happen, too many times."

"My parents?" Mal asked.

"No," Dagmara answered. She was even taller than her charge, and reached down to brush a strand of hair from the younger woman's eyes. "They avoided that trap."

Mal thought for a moment. "You didn't come here to watch me spar," she said.

"No, I did not," Dagmara said. "We received a report from PRUE."

PRUE was the sophisticated AI that assisted their crime-fighting community, the **P**olychannel **R**adiocommunications **U**nderstanding **E**ngine.

Dagmara handed her phone to Mal. "There was an incident today at the museum," she told the girl. "It tracks with the Talisman."

"He hasn't been on anyone's radar in...years, has he?" Mal asked.

"No," Dagmara said. "He fought with Force Majestic, and was known to have trained many crimefighters in the years thereafter. Including your parents."

Mal read the report on the phone. It compiled information from news reports, police band communications the news didn't have access to, and direct captures from museum video cameras.

Mal couldn't help a smile. "And now he's back," she said.

"It may not be the original," Dagmara said. "He would be very old by now. And I think it curious that he – or someone wearing his colors – emerges at an incident involving high schoolers."

Mal nodded. "And my high school, at that," she said. "I had Mrs. Cason last year. She's awesome. If nothing else, I'm relieved she's OK."

"Perhaps you should keep an eye out?" Dagmara said. "Pay extra attention at your school, and in the hallways."

Mal nodded. Then she glanced at the case that held her black and gray, carbon-fiber battle suit. "And if anything suspicious turns up, maybe Ms. Risk should look into it."

Chapter Seven

Saint Felix, like most cities its size, had its share of industrial districts. Some years they were busier than others, given the ups and downs of the global economy. This year was a good year, so those districts were seeing a great deal of traffic, of comings and goings, as manufacturing and storage and shipping all saw increases.

This made it easier to mask an operation that had nothing to do with industry.

The warehouse had a nondescript exterior, looking very like all the other warehouses around it, with its corrugated metal walls somewhere between boring gray and bland beige, as indistinct in daylight as in the moonlight that bathed it now.

But inside things were very different.

Men and women, tall and fit and focused, in matching black fatigues, went about their missions, even this deep in the night, engaging in planning, training, exercise, and even rest.

Prefab walls divided the building into a number of distinct areas. There were barracks, storage supply rooms, training areas, offices, and the War Room, the circular planning area which served as the nerve center for the operation, and where their leader currently attempted to gather his thoughts.

General Nicolas Talin paced the War Room. The super had tagged him at the museum. He wasn't seriously hurt, but he was still in some pain, and besides, it was embarrassing.

Talin tried to cope with his anger. Anger could, of course, be useful. It was good fuel, and burned clean and bright.

But it could also cloud judgement, and make a man less effective, blunting a sharp edge into uselessness.

His day had not gone according to plan.

The mission at the museum went badly sideways. It should have been, not a milk run, but a chance to keep the wits and skills of his people sharp with minimal risk while obtaining items vital to the success of the mission and throwing local law enforcement into a panic.

And then a damn super hero had shown up…!

He had known about Saint Felix's super hero community. The key to making his plan work could only be found in Saint Felix, and besides, a city of this size or greater usually had a super hero community. It simply wasn't avoidable. Dealing with super heroes was a necessary part of the plan.

He had planned the museum mission around the known patterns of the town's supers, the times and places they were known to operate. There shouldn't have been any interference…

Talin stopped dead in his tracks. *Which meant the super at the museum was a new player.*

But that didn't track.

The super at the museum had worn the colors of The Talisman, who had been a member of the supers community for ages but hadn't been active in more years than he had been on the scene in the first place.

Which meant, in turn, that this new Talisman had to be a legacy super hero.

"Crap," Talin said to himself.

Legacies were inexperienced, out to prove themselves, at least at the beginning. Which made them unpredictable, as likely to immolate themselves by accident as actually fight crime.

Talin shook his head. There was no way to anticipate how this Talisman would impact the plan, if at all, and therefore no reason to change it. He would brief his people on the possibilities. They were already the best, they could handle changing conditions.

He sat down in his chair at head of the conference table and pressed the intercom button. "Kessler, Moon, to the conference center," he said, his British accent clipped and distinct.

In moments the two men entered the room.

Talin wasted no time. "You're both familiar with the debacle at the museum today," Talin began.

Kessler and Moon each nodded.

"We're still proceeding as planned," Talin continued. "We obtained the fragment despite the interference of the new player. Moon, I trust you're prepared to proceed with the next element of the Ritual?'

Moon nodded, his pale face betraying nothing like a human feeling. "I'll begin the incantations immediately, General," he said, his voice low and deceptively soothing.

Talin turned to Kessler. "Can you stay on schedule, Dr. Kessler?" he asked.

Kessler stroked his goatee, thinking. Finally, he nodded. "As long as the other elements of the plan are properly executed? Yes," he answered.

"There may be a new super to contend with," Talin said. "Are you prepared for that variable?"

Kessler smiled. "I'm not concerned about any of that breed," he said.

Talin didn't smile, but he finally seemed satisfied. "We will achieve our objectives," he said.

"And then Sparta Eternal will rise."

Chapter Eight

Barton knocked on Nathan's front door. Nathan's dad answered.

"Barton!" he said. He reached out and grasped Barton in an enormous bear hug. For a moment Barton thought he was going to suffocate in the man's awe-inspiring beard, but then he found himself free.

Barton took a deep breath. "Hey, Mr. Saltzman," he said.

"Boy, you guys had a hell of a day yesterday!" Mr. Saltzman said.

"Yeah," Barton replied. "It was pretty frightening."

"I'm just glad no one was hurt," Nathan's father continued. "Come on in."

Barton entered his friend's home. He'd always felt welcome here, and enjoyed his visits, taking pleasure in perusing the array of rock and roll mementoes displayed on every available surface: tour posters, framed collections of ticket stubs, LP cover art, and more.

"Nathan's downstairs," his dad said. "In the game room. I imagine you and him have a lot to talk over."

Barton couldn't help smiling. "That would be an understatement."

Nathan sat on the great overstuffed couch in the downstairs game room. His hair was a mess and he still had on pajamas as Barton came down the stairs, making sure the door was closed behind him.

"Did you just wake up?" Barton asked as he paced the room.

"Yep," Nathan said. He rubbed at eyes that were half closed. "I was exhausted. Wrung out. Mom didn't like it, but Dad let me stay home today."

"My Mom kept me and Lucy home today, too," Barton said. Then he grew quiet. "Are we secure down here?" Barton asked.

Nathan's eyes snapped open. "Op-sec is good," he said. "Mom would eavesdrop, but Dad's working at home today. He wanted someone to be here in case I needed to talk."

Barton nodded.

They were quiet for a moment.

Then both of them began babbling over each other.

"Did you see-"

"Golden armor!"

"Tossed that guy like a –"

"Super-hero!"

Barton spilled everything to Nathan, including the dream-visit from Spooner. For a moment they were both out of breath.

"You're a superhero," Nathan said.

"Hold on a minute," Barton said. "I have this medallion. And I have powers. We haven't determined I'm gonna be a superhero yet."

Nathan just looked at him. Barton smiled with glee.

"Yes! Yes, I'm a superhero!" he said, unable to contain himself. "But what am I gonna do about it?"

"I'm the only person that knows, right?" Nathan asked.

"Right," Barton replied.

"You can trust me," Nathan said. "I'll keep your secret identity on pain of death."

"I know," Barton said.

"Are you gonna go on patrol?" Nathan said.

"Is that what supers do?" Barton asked. "Leap from rooftops and beat up muggers? I don't think I can do that. I don't have a car and as far as I can tell, I can't fly, so I don't have a way to get places on my own."

"That's problematic, then," Nathan said. "Is there a welcoming committee? Do other supers come to you? Is there a handbook?"

"Not that I can find," Barton said. "I couldn't get back to sleep after the dream, so I spent hours searching. Superheroes must be pretty good at keeping details about their lives off the internet, is all I can say."

"Did you find anything about Spooner?" Nathan asked. "You know, from before he was a super."

"Not yet," Barton said. "But I'm gonna keep looking."

Nathan smiled and shook his head. "Wild," Nathan said. "Very Obi-Wan."

"I think I'm still having my origin story," Barton said. "What I do, how I do it, what the Talisman stands for, that's all still up in the air."

Barton sat down on the couch. "What about those guys at the museum?" he said. "The ones who attacked us."

"I had no idea who they were," Nathan said.

"Neither did I," Barton said. "But they were after those artifacts. They had serious support, helicopter extraction lined up, plenty of hardware," Barton said.

"It seems like a lot for a museum robbery," Nathan said.

"Yeah," Barton said. "Especially in broad daylight on a Monday. You could easily wait until night, sneak in, less chance of discovery."

"They needed those artifacts," Nathan said. "Badly enough that they couldn't wait."

"Who were they?" Barton asked.

Barton and Nathan each went to work. They scanned local and national TV news, and every online news source they could find. They found lots of stories about the mysterious super-heroic rescuer of the school kids at the museum, but nothing about the identities of the attackers.

"We aren't the FBI," Barton said. "We don't have the resources to track these guys down on our own."

"Where do we start, then?" Nathan said.

Barton thought. "Mrs. Cason," he said. "It's the artifacts. There's something more to them than just their history. And she'll know what it is."

Chapter Nine

Barton rolled out of bed Wednesday morning, excited, active, and ready to go. This annoyed Lucy and made their mother suspicious. But Mrs. Harper put the suspicion aside and just counted her blessings that at least one of her children was eager to get to school that day.

Barton bounded out of the SUV in front of Leiter Memorial High School with a smile on his face, waving to his mom and sister as they pulled away.

"Love you!" his mom called, waving.

"You suck!" his sister called, waving.

Barton walked into the school's lobby, which was jammed with a surging mass of teenage humanity. He immediately picked out Nathan. They linked up and made their way through the crowd into the depths of their high school.

The walked into Mrs. Cason's room. Her social studies class was normally their first class of the day, but she was still surprised to see them.

"You two are never early," she said. She crossed her arms and arched an eyebrow. "What's going on?"

Nathan and Barton exchanged a glance, each trying hard to look innocent. "Nothing, Mrs. Cason," Nathan said.

"We just wanted to ask more about the exhibit from Monday," Barton said.

After a moment, Mrs. Cason's face softened. "What do you want to know?" she asked.

"Well," Barton began, "we knew at least it would be interesting, because you would never take us to something boring."

"Suck up," Mrs. Cason said.

"Is it working?" Barton asked.

"Little bit," Cason said.

"Good," Barton said. "But no one was expecting a full-bore action movie robbery scene Monday. So I guess I'm asking, is there something about this exhibit, those artifacts, we should know?"

Mrs. Cason thought for a moment. "Not exactly," she said. "They're interesting, but it's not like they're forged in gold and platinum or encased in precious gems or anything. Mostly they're interesting to historians and social studies teachers."

She took a moment, turned to her desk, and grabbed her coffee mug. She took a sip.

"Some of the pieces in the exhibit have an interesting past, though," she said. "A British team was running an excavation near Athens back around 1900 or so. They loaded their spoils, journeyed to the nearest port, and prepared to make their way back to London. One of the lead archaeologists on the team had a premonition, a nightmare, that they should not have disturbed…something."

"Should not have disturbed what, exactly?" Nathan asked.

"No idea," Mrs. Cason continued. "The ship was caught in a storm and sank in the Mediterranean. All hands lost. The whole team drowned before he could write down what they shouldn't have disturbed."

"So how did these artifacts come to be here?" Barton asked.

"Vance Solutions," Mrs. Cason said.

A light went on for Barton. "Terry Vance. The inventor," he said. "Early cell network engineering, work on space travel, medical advances – you name it."

"All of which made Vance stupidly rich," Mrs. Cason said. "And allowed him the time and money to indulge his whims – I mean, his interests."

She took a sip of coffee. "He led a dive to the wreck of the ship last year and brought the artifacts back," she said. "He donated them to the Saint Felix museum and here we are."

"What did we miss?" Barton asked.

"There were your classic vases, pottery, statues, artworks," Mrs. Cason said. "Plates. Stoneware. Jewelry."

Inside, Barton sighed. None of that sounded worth a high-stakes caper.

"And there were fragments of other things," she went on. "Weapons, swords and shields, that sort of thing. A legend grew up, over the decades, that some of those items, even broken, carried some element of magic or power. It's fun to think about."

Then she snorted. "But nobody really believes any of that," she said.

Somebody believes it, Barton thought. *Enough to stage that robbery.*

"Is there anything else I can help you with?" she continued. "Class starts soon."

Barton shook his head. "No, Ma'am," he said. "I'm good,"

"I could use some extra credit," Nathan said.

"Try turning in your work," Mrs. Cason answered.

Before Nathan could continue, a knock came at the door. They all turned to see a tall girl there, with blond hair pulled harshly back and an intense look on her face.

"Good morning, Mrs. Cason," she said.

"Good morning, Mal," Mrs. Cason answered. "How can I help you?"

"I wanted to see if you were OK," Mal answered. "I bet Monday was pretty intense."

"Yeah, it was," she said. "But I'll be OK. Boys, this is Mallory Savage, I had her in class last year."

Barton and Nathan were momentarily stunned into silence. Barton spurred himself to action first. "Hey," he said. "Call me Bart."

Mal paid him no attention. "Glad you're OK, Mrs. Cason," she said as she left.

Nathan looked to Barton. "What about Courtney?" he asked.

"Courtney who?" Barton said.

Chapter Ten

Mal walked the halls of Leiter High, heading to the cafeteria. She observed the surging mass of students around her. Some had their ear buds in, listening to music from their phones, disconnected from the world. Others talked to friends, or simply looked worried, lost in their thoughts.

What are they worried about? Mal thought. *Tests? Boys? Girls? Their parents?*

She shook her head. After the places she'd been and the things she had seen and done as Ms. Risk, the concerns of these kids seemed so…small. So ordinary.

But Dagmara had cautioned her against that. It was these ordinary people and all the others like them that people with powers and masks sought to defend, that they could live out their ordinary lives in peace and happiness.

Mal looked around. She didn't have one friend among these ordinary people. *I wonder if it would help if I knew anyone here beyond a name or a face?* she thought.

But she did have out-of-the-ordinary friends. She was about to have lunch with them.

She sat down at their regular table, a far distance from the other students, near the huge windows. She had pizza, of course. Pizza Day at the school cafeteria was kind of a big deal.

Mal looked around the table. Everyone was present and accounted for.

Colin Ballard shoveled pizza in as fast as he could.

Paris Paxton ate with a knife and fork, delicately and neatly.

Tucker Alexander, his smooth-skinned brown head gleaming in the sunlight, ate a slice with movements as precise as a ballet.

She knew who they were and what they could do outside this school. Did they want out as badly as she did, to pursue their other lives full time? She would have to ask them, as soon as she figured out how.

"Hey, Mal," Colin said though a mouthful of pizza. "How you doing?"

Mal shrugged. "I think I passed my science test," she said.

Paris smiled brightly. "I'm pretty sure I aced it," she said. "Not even a challenge."

"How could it be a challenge, for you?" Tucker asked, in his slight, musical accent.

Mal ate her pizza and drank her apple juice. She breathed easy for a moment, enjoying the company of her friends.

Paris thought for a moment. "I suppose you're right," she said. "But I still like to execute, you know? I'm gunning for valedictorian."

Colin chuckled. "You'll have to beat me for it," he said.

"No powers, Colin," Paris said. "If you want to make this a whole thing between us, fine. But we do it fair and square."

"Your brain is your power, Paris," Colin said.

"Colin," she said, a warning in her voice.

Colin put up is hands. "No powers. A deal is a deal," he said. "But I'm still gonna win."

Paris smiled, sunny and bright. "We'll see," she said.

Mal swallowed a bite. "I think I have him," she said.

Her friends grew quiet.

"Who?" Tucker asked.

"The Talisman," Mal said.

They leaned in.

"I studied the Talisman's body language in the cell phone and security footage of the incident," Mal continued.

"Are we sure this is the Talisman?" Tucker asked.

"It's the same mystical energy as the original," Colin said. "My spell from last night confirms that."

"Then that means it's a new wielder," Tucker said.

"I went to visit Mrs. Cason this morning, to see if I could find out anything about the Museum attack Monday," Mal said. "A pair of her sophomores were in there, talking to her."

"Did you know them?" Paris asked.

"One of them was Nathan Saltzman," Mal said. "You know, the rocker kid?"

Paris made a face. "Kind of a weirdo," she said.

"The other one was Barton Harper," Mal went on. "It's him."

Her friends looked at her, astonished.

"Surely you jest," Tucker said.

"Mallory, sweetie…" Paris started.

Only Colin remained silent.

Mal raised her hands, insistent. "It's him," she said. "The way he moves. Unmistakable. Like someone who's never had that kind of power before."

Quiet fell over the table.

"How did it happen?" Paris said. "How did a…a….rando like Barton Harper become the Talisman?"

"More to the point," Mal said, "what's he going to do with it? And what does he know about the robbery?"

"We're going to have to bring him in," Colin finally said.

After a moment, Mal nodded. "Colin's right," she said. "Meet at my place at 8pm tonight and we'll plan our next move."

"It's not just that," Colin said. "Last night's spell showed me something else. There's a second force in Saint Felix right now. Something dark, malevolent.

"And we may need the extra muscle sooner rather than later."

Chapter Eleven

Cindy Lauren opened her eyes. It took a few moments for her to come fully awake, and she immediately wished she hadn't. She lay on a rough wooden platform, a couple of feet above a cold stone floor in a windowless room with a wooden door. She tried to move, but discovered she was bound by broad leather straps.

Panic began to rise in her. The last thing she remembered was leaving work on Tuesday night. She had worked late at the boutique, Carrie had called in sick, someone had to close. She volunteered, which was stupid, because she had to get home, Peter was expecting her, he needed help studying for a test. She locked up, was making her way to her car, fumbling in the humid darkness

for the car keys in her purse when she heard footsteps. Then –
nothing.

Until waking up here.

"Hello?" she said. "Can anyone hear me?"

An echo was her only response.

"Hello?" she cried, even louder. "Hello? Help! Please,
someone help me!"

She burst into tears. Her face was soon slick with them,
unable as she was to even wipe them away.

She cried for help another time, then another, her cries
finally becoming little more than inarticulate wails.

Then she fell silent, her throat too raw to scream.

She waited, her stomach churning, breathing in short gasps.

Finally, she heard the sound of a key in a lock. She
whipped her head up to see the wooden door creak open.

A man entered. He didn't seem crazy, or at first glance
even especially threatening. Middle aged, average height. A white
dress shirt and khakis. A leather bag slung over one shoulder. A
pale face, framed by slicked-back black hair.

But then she saw the eyes. And knew that she was in terrible danger.

He smiled at her. "Welcome," he said. "Please have the satisfaction of knowing you are essential to our plan."

"What plan?" she croaked out. "Who are you?"

"Our plan?" he asked. "Our plan is to rise up and show the world a better way of being." The man paused. "Well, that's the General's plan, anyway. I expect to be well compensated for my assistance."

Cindy felt confused. "Money?" she said. "You want money? That's why you're doing this?"

The man crossed the room and stood by her. He unslung the bag from his shoulder and laid it gently on the floor. "I said compensated," the man pointed out. "There are forms of compensation beyond simply filthy money."

"Who are you?" she asked. "Where am I? Why did you bring me here?'

The man paused for a moment. "I'll answer your questions," he said. "Since it's exceedingly unlikely you'll ever be able to tell anyone about this."

He began to roll up his sleeves, revealing arms full of tattoos, of snakes, bats, and other, worse things she couldn't name.

"My name is Miles Moon," he said. "Although you won't find that name in any database or filing cabinet. I've spent my life learning the darkest magic."

She watched as he began gesturing with his hands. Energy began to crackle in and around his fingers.

"You are in a secret basement somewhere in Saint Felix," he continued. "A hidden place, where I can conduct my rituals in privacy."

His arms began to move in wider arcs as the energy crackled even more. Then the tattoos on his arms began to glow.

She was too scared to scream.

"And I brought you here," he continued, his voice glacially calm and controlled, "because the rituals led me to you. You see, you're the most suited, in the whole city. So that your energy, your very life force, might fuel our efforts."

A sound like thunder roared. In the confined space of the room it was painful to hear, and Cindy flinched in agony. If Moon even noticed, he didn't show it. He was too focused on his terrible task.

A glowing sphere appeared, floating about two feet above Cindy. It spun rapidly, spitting energy.

Moon stopped his motions, arms resting at his sides, and he smiled. "We're ready," he said. "You should be excited. We're going to make history."

He reached down and opened the bag at his feet. He pulled from it a broken, shattered sword, only a hilt with a fragment of blade, green and tarnished with age.

"It's called the Scythe of Cronos," Moon said. "It is a source of great power. What's left of it, anyway. And though this ritual will take some time, your energy will open the doorway to its power."

Moon held the sword up, and it leapt from his hand into the sphere. Cindy had time for one strangled scream before her voice grew quiet. Her eyes turned white as tendrils of life-energy curled from her face and her hands to the sword itself.

Moon smiled. The transfer was working flawlessly. Pity about the woman, but then there was that old saying about omelets and eggs. And the General would be very happy, indeed.

Chapter Twelve

Colin Ballard slouched off the school bus and onto the sidewalk in front of his home, backpack heavy on his shoulders. He had no need of these mundane things, of course, but took a certain pleasure in their normalcy. The smell of the bus's exhaust, the sweat and bad breath on the bus, the unusually warm day for October in Saint Felix, all in their own way grounded him.

He looked at his home, to all appearances a normal three-story townhouse in a row of townhouses. He walked up the flagstone path to his front door. He pulled the key from his pocket, placed it in the lock, and opened the door. He slipped inside.

The cool air was a shock after the hot day, but a welcome one. The rows upon rows of bookshelves, the shadowy hallway, the dark paneling, and the thick carpet seemed a world away from the rest of his life.

He walked to the kitchen and pulled a soda from the refrigerator. He opened it, took a drink, closed his eyes, let his awareness flow out from his center.

He opened his eyes again, and the pale, translucent shade of his father was there.

"Hello, Colin," said Bailey Ballard.

"Hey, Dad," said Colin.

"I can only speak for a moment," said Bailey. "The veil is more resistant today."

Colin felt a prickle at the base of his neck. "Could that mean trouble?" he asked.

"It very well might," said Bailey.

"I'll look into it right away," Colin said. "I love you, Dad."

Bailey's eyes seemed to mist over. "I love you too, son," he said. "I'll find my way back. I swear it."

And then he was gone.

Colin draw a hand across his eyes. "I'm not crying, you're crying," he said to no one in particular. And then he took a deep breath and headed towards the stairs.

As he walked upstairs he draw his hand in a signature fashion across his clothing, and his school wear dissolved into his favorite black suit, with a black shirt and matching black silk tie. It was a bit much for high schooler Colin Ballard.

But it was just right for the Mysteriad.

Colin took his father's call sign when he went to work. The Mysteriad was known to but a few, but Colin drew confidence from the name, wore it almost like armor.

The door to the Study opened as he approached. The books that lined these walls were even older, some in languages that had not been spoken aloud on earth in eons.

The lectern in the middle of the study had a velvet cloth over it, upon which rested a lump of ancient quartz. The quartz – called the Locus - glowed, casting golden highlights on the room.

Mysteriad's blood ran cold.

He stepped up to the quartz, and commanded, "Show me."

Shades of light flashed over the quartz, and hums and whispers of sound could be heard. Mysteriad knew how to read and listen to these signs, and they spoke of nothing good.

He turned from the quartz and paced the room, drawing a hand through tousled black hair. The Locus had detected power, dark power, unleashed in Saint Felix.

It was more power than Colin had seen since taking up the name of the Mysteriad, since his father had been...had been lost.

Mysteriad calmed himself. He was far from alone. There were other mages in his father's circles he could contact for help. There were all the books around him, knowledge spanning millennia. He had his own friends that he could face this with, Mal and Paris and Tucker.

He pulled on the lapels of his suit and straightened his tie.

He was not without his own powers, for that matter.

He turned back to the Locus. With a simple incantation, the lights and sounds over the Locus grew ordered. It was a technique his father had taught him, back in the beginning, a way to organize the flow of energy from the Locus into something more understandable.

"I like to think of it as an Excel document for magic," his father had said.

Mysteriad shook his head. For a sorcerer his father could be a dork. But he wasn't wrong. He could read the energy from the Locus better this way.

He could see, for example, that the dark power unleashed in Saint Felix had come from one sorcerer. He could tell that it had been focused through a magical artifact of some kind.

And he could tell that it had come at the cost of an innocent life.

He could feel the rage rising in his heart. If there was anything he and his father and all their friends stood for, it was for protecting the innocent.

He would discover what he could. He would take that information to his friends.

And together, whatever was going on, they would put a stop to it.

Chapter Thirteen

The scanning beam reached past her striking pale blue eyes to examine the retinas behind them. A moment passed, then two, and the indicator light turned from red to green and Paris Paxton walked through the airlock into her workshop.

Sensors detected her presence, causing automated systems to activate monitors and boot up computers. Lights sprung to life, illuminating her red G-Girl coverall in its case and her ship, the Pod, in its cradle.

She slung her backpack on a chair. Homework could wait. The attack at the museum, the emergence of a new Talisman... Something was afoot in Saint Felix. She felt it in her gut.

She sat down at her main workstation and began bringing up data.

"Computer," she said, "start Playlist Zero Five."

The sound of seventies rock and roll filled her workshop as her fingers played across her keyboard. What should she even look for? Instinct was a fine thing, but by itself couldn't solve crimes much beyond lost dog cases, if that.

She knew somewhere Colin was examining the mystical side of things. Whatever it was that had brought the Talisman back, if it was really Barton Harper, that would have to be the job of someone else on the team. Her specialties lay elsewhere.

That business at the museum was troublesome. Guns, ammunition, even the helicopters were easy enough to get your hands on. Personnel could be found without much trouble – there was always someone looking for a cause, or just to get paid.

She wracked her brains. Could she track shipping manifests? Were there records of power consumption she could access?

Paris decided she needed coffee.

She rose from her workstation and went back though the airlock and up the stairs.

Paris entered the kitchen. She went straight to work, putting water and grounds and a filter into the coffee maker. She went to the refrigerator, and pulled out the half and half and waited. The sounds and smells of the coffee maker working were almost a ritual for her, something soothing, as much a part of the experience as the jolt of the caffeine. As she waited she wondered idly what time her parents would be home, wondered what was for dinner, what she would take for lunch at school tomorrow…

The maker finished its work. She removed the pot, poured a mug, added the half and half, and inhaled the steam and the aroma as she gently carried the coffee back down to her workshop. She repeated the retinal scan, reentered the airlock to find her equipment operating just as she had left it.

She sat back down at her workstation, took a sip of the hot coffee, and then it hit her.

The helicopters.

It was hard to hide helicopters in broad daylight.

"Duh," she said.

She went to work, accessing the files of the Saint Felix Police, looking for the feeds from the traffic cameras outside the museum from the time of the attack on Monday.

There was nothing.

There were video files leading up to the attack, and after it was over. But nothing of the actual event.

Smart, she thought. *They disabled these feeds before they even started.*

Paris then began looking at video feeds from the streets around the museum, and leading to it, in the hour before and the hour after. She found nothing, no footage of the choppers from any angle, no sense of where they had come from or where they had gone. Whoever had planned this op had been very thorough.

Something, though…something tickled at the back of her brain. Something she couldn't quite put her finger on…

She walked over to the holotable.

She'd designed and built it herself. It was about 4 feet by 6 feet, with custom state of the art holoprojectors and interactivity.

She hadn't shown it to Mal yet, because Mal would want one for the townhouse but she had absolutely no time to build another one right now and for sure wasn't giving this one up.

"Computer," she said, "access holomap of Saint Felix."

A ghostly green dimensional projection of her city rose from the holotable.

"Computer, transfer information on deactivated traffic cameras to map. Mark the map by the streets of the deactivated cameras."

And there it was, plain as day. Someone had been clever enough to deactivate the traffic cameras to avoid the choppers being photographed. But Paris could follow the path of those deactivations through the map of the city.

Her eyes tracked the route she was now sure the choppers had taken. It ended in one of Saint Felix's industrial districts, where there were fewer cameras and thus no more route to follow.

But she and her team now had a very place to start looking.

Chapter Fourteen

Tucker Alexander opened the extraordinarily heavy wood double doors that led into his home. Someone with baseline human strength would have found it difficult, if not impossible. It was an extra layer of security, one that would escape notice.

Of course, he was far from baseline human. He reflected again, as he had many times before, how easy this world of ordinary humans was to navigate compared to where he had come from. His speed and strength made many things easier.

He passed through the foyer into the living room. "Mr. Vance?" he called, his deep voice booming in the corridors of his home. "Terry?"

Hearing no response, he tossed his bag onto the sofa and headed through the living room into and past the dining room into the kitchen. He looked around. "Ms. Carlin?" he called after the housekeeper. Again, he heard no response.

Shrugging, he went to the refrigerator and pulled out the makings of a massive sandwich, turkey and ham and cheese and tomato and green pepper and mustard…

He heard the echo of the front doors opening and closing and the whir of an electric motor. He quickly closed the stainless-steel doors of the fridge, assembled his sandwich, and walked towards the living room

Terry Vance rolled in just as Tucker came in the other side of the living room. Terry saw the sandwich and couldn't suppress a broad smile. "Hungry?" he asked.

"Just a snack," Tucker said through a mouthful of sandwich.

Terry steered his chair through the living room to Tucker's side, where he clapped a dark brown hand on the younger man's arm. "Good to see you," he said. "How was school today?"

Tucker swallowed. "It was alright," he said. "Mal thinks she knows who the new Talisman is."

Terry's eyes got wide. "That's a bold claim," he said. "What's her theory?'

"She thinks it's a sophomore named Barton Harper," Tucker continued. "He would have been on the field trip that got stuck in the middle of that museum robbery on Monday."

Terry nodded. "What's she got?" he asked.

"She said she observed his body language at school and compared it to video of the attack," Tucker said. "We're looking into it."

Tucker got a strange look on his face. "Did you know him?" he asked. "The original Talisman?'

"I met him once or twice," Terry said. "He was a part of the generation before mine. He trained them, fought with them. My band of heroes came later, and he had moved on to…whatever other things drove him."

He drew a hand across his dark beard, his eyes for a moment seeming like they were somewhere else. "We fought in one of those big battles that draws us all together periodically," Terry said. "There was something about him...something older, somehow, like something from a different time. But I couldn't put my finger on it. And we were never close."

"If it is this Harper kid, how did he get picked?" Tucker asked.

"I couldn't tell you," Terry said. "But there was something about the Talisman...I researched his history once or twice. I never found anything conclusive, but I think there may be deep, deep history there."

"Speaking of history," Tucker went on, around bites of sandwich, "can you tell me anything about the exhibit?"

"I just got back from the museum," he said. "We were evaluating the damage to the artifacts on display – Tucker, we're going to the kitchen, I'm getting hungry watching you eat."

Terry steered his chair, electric engine humming quietly, to the kitchen. He opened the stainless-steel doors of the refrigerator and rummaged through its contents, settling on a thick slice of Chicago-style pizza that he proceeded to eat cold.

"Ever since you to came to live with me, you've been eating me out of house and home," Terry said around mouthfuls of pizza. "Poor Ms. Carlin has to go to the grocery twice, sometimes three times a week."

Another smile crossed his rugged features. "Good thing I'm rich."

He finished the pizza. "The interesting thing about the museum," he said, "is that while the attackers caused a lot of damage, made a lot of noise, they only made off with one thing."

Tucker arched an eyebrow.

"The Scythe of Cronos," Terry said. "In terms of money, it's the least valuable of the lot. There's no reason to stage an attack like that and make off with only a broken hunk of sword.

"Unless there's more to it."

A shadow seemed to pass over Terry's eyes. "This could be nothing," he said. "An overfunded bunch of commando cosplayers with more money than sense who followed a half-baked legend and will end up empty handed.

"Or...they could know something we don't," he finished.

"We're gathering tonight at Mal's townhouse," Tucker said. "Paris and Colin are doing their things. We might have some more to go on soon."

Terry nodded. "Good," he said. "But be careful. And don't be afraid to signal for help if you need it."

Tucker smiled. "Don't worry," he said. "We've got it covered."

And with that, he grabbed an apple, bit into it, and left the kitchen.

Terry smiled and shook his head. He'd been that optimistic, once. Hell, who was he kidding? Even after everything that had happened, he still was. *That's why Tucker and I get along so well,* he thought.

But he hoped the boy had some sense of self-preservation. He'd hate to take bad news back to Tucker's mother…

Chapter Fifteen

April Harper hit the driveway at 6:30 pm on the nose, a trio of loaded sub sandwiches on the seat beside her. The week had been stressful, and it was only Wednesday, so take-out it was.

She entered the house, kicked off her shoes, and immediately heard the sound of Barton playing video games in the living room. "Hey, mom!" Barton called. "How was the office today?"

"Tiring," Mrs. Harper replied. "The client on the county history book fails to understand we can't keep our deadlines if he can't keep his."

She entered the living room and sat down on the couch next to Barton, placing the sandwiches on the coffee table. Barton paused his game and sorted through the stack for his sandwich.

"It's your favorite," April said. "Meatball and Tuna with extra pickle."

Barton found his sandwich, opened the paper, and took a huge bite. He chewed with a look of intense pleasure on his face.

Lucy bounded down the stairs and gave April a tight hug. "Thanks for dinner, Mom," she said. "If it was up to Barton we'd probably starve."

Barton considered this. "She's not wrong," he said through a mouthful of sandwich.

Mrs. Harper ate her sandwich – turkey with extra tomato – and Lucy hers – ham with cheese and green peppers. Lucy complained about her day – no one at school was talking about the Monday attack anymore. She still had things to say, but no one in third grade was listening.

Barton talked a little about his conversation with Mrs. Cason, then brought something up with his mother.

"I know it's a school night," he began, "but Nathan's asked me to go to a movie with him. It's a documentary about his favorite band, playing down at the Capital tonight."

Mrs. Harper swallowed a bite. "School night," she said. "Plus, I'm stressed out enough as it is."

"Please, Mom?" Barton asked. "All you have to do is drop me off. Nathan's dad will pick us up and bring us home."

Lucy looked at her mom. "It would give us some time to get caught up on our shows," she said.

Mrs. Harper looked reluctant, but finally nodded her head. "OK," she said. "But I don't want any trouble getting you up for school tomorrow."

The night was warm and dry as Mrs. Harper dropped Barton off in front of the theater. Nathan was already there waiting. "I've got tickets for the nine o'clock show," he called.

"You two stay out of trouble, OK?" Mrs. Harper said through the open passenger side window of her SUV.

"You bet, Mrs. Harper!" Nathan said. "My week has been exciting enough as it is!"

Lucy waved from the back seat, and called out to Nathan, "Eat some popcorn for me!" as her mom drove away.

Barton looked at Nathan. "Have you noticed she's not abusive to you?" Barton asked.

Nathan shrugged. "I am demonstrably cooler than you," he said.

"So, how are we gonna do this?" Barton asked.

Nathan looked around. "Down that alley," he said.

The boys moved quickly down the sidewalk and entered a secluded alleyway. They each looked around.

"No security cameras," Barton said.

"No windows. No people with cell phones," Nathan said.

Barton nodded. He pulled the medallion out of his shirt. "I hope this works," he said.

He stood there for a minute.

"What do I do?" Barton asked.

"Beats me," Nathan said.

Barton took a moment to think, then grasped the medallion in his hand. He closed his eyes and focused on it.

When he opened his eyes, he was again clad in the gold-and-black of the Talisman.

"Dang," Nathan said. "It was like you…morphed, or something. One instant I'm looking at Barton, the next I'm looking at the Talisman."

Barton stretched his arms and his neck. "I can feel it," he said. "The difference. It's not like a bolt of lightning or anything. It's more like…a hum in the back of my mind. I can feel what I can do."

"Speaking of which," Nathan said, "what's the plan?"

"We head to the museum," Barton said. "I'm betting there's a clue, some hint as to what's going on."

Barton looked around. He saw a fire escape. "There," he said. "I'll climb up there and head across the rooftops. The museum is only three or four blocks from here."

Nathan coughed.

"Oh," Barton said.

The two boys stood there for a minute.

"Well," Barton said, "climb on."

"No," Nathan said.

"You'd rather stay behind?" Barton said.

"It's undignified," Nathan said.

"No one's supposed to see us anyway," Barton said.

Nathan stood there for a moment.

"Fine," he said. "But this doesn't make me your sidekick."

Nathan puts his arms around Barton's shoulders. Barton approached the fire escape, reached for it, and in moments was racing up it, carrying Nathan on his back.

Chapter Sixteen

Mal Savage entered a code sequence into the keypad. The case slid open with a quiet whoosh and revealed the black and gray body armor she wore in her other identity.

Mal dressed in the armor, her uniform. It was sleek, form fitting and flexible. The basic design had been developed by one of Terry Vance's companies and he was, in his own words, "more than happy" to assist the next generation of Saint Felix's supers stay safe while learning on the job.

Finished with the change, she looked in a mirror. Mal Savage wasn't looking back.

She was Miss Risk.

The basement level was for her training. The top floor of the townhouse was for meetings.

It wasn't as elaborate as the professional supers had access to, but Miss Risk still loved it. The round table with its chairs for each member of their group, the wide screen monitors with their news feeds so they could keep an eye on trouble in the city, and the real-time uplink to the PRUE AI all made her feel like she was in charge of something real.

She walked up the stairs to access the roof and wait for her friends. Night had fallen, but the warmth of the day still lingered. Saint Felix was never truly quiet, but up here, after dark, she could think just a little bit better.

Her friends were due. They were all late, of course.

But one by one, they arrived.

A low hum heralded the approach of the Pod. The Pod was a hovercraft, an egg-shaped vehicle designed by Paris Paxton to transport their team. It landed on the roof, but Paris was in her work clothes when she stepped out – she wore her own uniform, the pouch-laden coverall of her alter-ego, G-Girl.

A puff of blue smoke, and another friend arrived. During the day, in school, she knew him as Colin Ballard. But here in the night, with his hair slicked back and wearing one of the black suits he favored, he was the Mysteriad.

And as if from nowhere, leaping across from another building, was Tucker Alexander, known by the name the Athenian, in her trademark chain mail tunic and domino mask.

Miss Risk smiled. At moments like this all her worries fell away. Nothing could bother her, nothing could stop her. She was with her friends.

She was with the Danger Patrol.

They took their seats around the table and began to make their reports.

"There's a sorcerer at work in Saint Felix," Mysteriad said. "Someone accessing dark energies. I believe an innocent life has been sacrificed for power. And they've used some kind of artifact to focus that power, to use it."

Mysteriad's voice trembled with rage. Miss Risk had seen this in him before, his respect for life and his anger at the waste of it.

"I'm not sure where they are," he continued, "or what they plan on doing. But I can feel it in the air, like a dark rain."

He could also be a little dramatic. But Miss Risk thought that might be the cost of doing business for a teenage sorcerer.

"I may have a lead about that artifact," Athenian said, his deep voice echoing in the meeting room even as he attempted to speak quietly. "I spoke with Mr. Vance about it. Even after all the trouble of the attack, the thieves only captured one item. It's called the Scythe of Cronos."

"What does it do?" Miss Risk asked.

"Mr. Vance wasn't sure," Athenian replied. "In terms of money, it was the least valuable of the lot. But he allowed as they might know something we don't."

"I've got an idea about them," G-Girl said. "I've been analyzing data from traffic cameras and other video sources. I have a hunch about where our unsubs might be."

G-Girl touched a panel at her place at the table, activating the data link between her lab and their meeting room. A map of Saint Felix appeared on one of the room's monitors.

"The choppers that helped the unsubs flee the scene headed for our warehouse district, specifically this cluster of warehouses on the east side," G-Girl said. "None of them are listed as currently occupied and none of them are drawing any power or other services from the city grid."

"So, we're just gonna have to go out there and do the legwork," Miss Risk said. She was rising from her chair when an alarm sounded.

"That's a motion detector," G-Girl said.

Athenian went to one of the monitors. A live video feed was displayed from the roof of the museum.

The Talisman was there!

"The warehouses will have to wait," Miss Risk said. "Everyone get aboard the Pod!"

Chapter Seventeen

Talisman and Nathan stood on the roof of the museum. The city spread out around them. They could see the glow of neon and hear the sounds of cars and sirens and all the bustle of the people below.

"This feels like being a superhero," Talisman said. "You know, rooftops at night, the glow of city lights, that kind of thing."

"I know what you mean," Nathan said. "I feel like I can fly."

"Let's get to work. We've got to find something before your dad comes to pick us up," Talisman said.

They prowled the rooftop, scouring every surface for anything to aid in their cause.

"I can't find anything," Talisman said.

"I thought this would be easier," Nathan said.

"Me too," said Talisman. "Like maybe there would be a note with a riddle, or the key to a locker at the airport, or a receipt to a coffee shop, or some kind of mud only found at one river in France."

"Or shell casings, or boot prints, or a splatter of blood," Nathan said.

"What would we do with any of those?" Talisman asked.

"I don't know," Nathan said. "Take them to the lab?"

"I don't have a lab," Talisman said. "I'm still pretty new at this in case you haven't noticed."

"I found something," Nathan said.

In an instant Talisman was at his side.

"What do you have?" he asked.

Nathan pointed at a small, unobtrusive piece of technology, a black device about the size and shape of an ink pen.

"It looks a lot like some kind of...pocket camera, maybe?" Nathan said.

They looked at each other.

"Someone knows we're here," Talisman said.

"I looked right at it," Nathan said. "I'm not wearing a mask. They're gonna know who I am and figure out who you are."

"Don't panic," Talisman said. "We don't know that yet."

"Do you hear that?" Nathan asked.

Talisman cocked his head. "That weird humming noise?" he said.

A sleek ovoid craft appeared over the side of the museum. It was silver and blue, with a tinted cockpit. A wash of air came over them from the ship's propulsion system.

"Crap!" Nathan said, and hid behind Talisman. "No mask!"

"ATTENTION TALISMAN," a voice from the craft said. "WE ARE THE DANGER PATROL. STAND DOWN. WE ARE PREPARING TO LAND."

"Stand down?" Talisman said. "We weren't doing anything."

The craft lowered landing gear and set down on the rooftop with a soft hiss. A hatch in the side slid open and a short ramp extended. A young woman in gray and black body armor walked down the ramp.

"I'm Miss Risk," she said. "We need to talk."

Talisman felt his heart begin to race. He struggled to find words.

"Are you the Talisman?" Miss Risk asked.

Talisman couldn't find any words.

"Barton!" Nathan whispered harshly from behind Talisman. "Say something!"

"Are...are you dating anyone?" Talisman asked.

Nathan sighed and shook his head.

"What was that?" Miss Risk asked with an edge in her voice.

"Nothing," Talisman said quickly. "Yes, I'm the Talisman."

"Are you the same individual who operated under that name in the seventies?" Miss Risk asked.

"I wasn't even born yet," Talisman answered.

"Are you prepared to answer why you're on this rooftop?" Miss Risk asked.

"We're looking for clues to the robbery from Monday," Talisman answered. "We haven't found anything, in case you were wondering."

Nathan coughed.

"Except for that little camera over there," Talisman said. "Which I'm guessing is yours?"

Miss Risk nodded.

"So, what happens now?" Talisman asked. "Do we fight or something? Maybe wrestle?"

Nathan punched Talisman in the shoulder.

"Who's that with you?" Miss Risk asked.

"No one," Talisman said.

Miss Risk shook her head.

"There's someone standing behind you," she said.

"That's...Talisman Boy," Talisman said.

Nathan punched him again.

"Talisman Boy?" Miss Risk said.

"That's not my name," Nathan called out. "I'm just here as an advisor."

"Could you come from behind Talisman?" Miss Risk called.

"No mask," Nathan said.

Miss Risk reached into a pouch on her uniform and pulled out a roll of gauze bandages. She tossed them in the air and they landed precisely beside Talisman.

"Will that do for now?" she asked.

Nathan picked up the bandages. He quickly unspooled them and wrapped them around his head. He emerged from behind Talisman. Miss Risk snickered.

"Close enough," she said. "That was our camera. Don't worry, we didn't see your faces. And even if we had, we would protect your identities. The Danger Patrol exists to help protect and train the next generation of Saint Felix's heroes."

"You're here to help?" Talisman asked.

"Yes," Miss Risk said. "Can you come with us?"

"Sure," said Talisman. "We just need to be back at 11 for our ride."

Chapter Eighteen

Talisman's stomach lurched as the pod lifted off from the roof. It got worse when the pod angled over the edge of the roof and took to the sky over Saint Felix.

He couldn't read Nathan at all. The bandages hid his expression well. The other young people in the pod with them acted undisturbed. *How often have they done this?* he wondered.

He grabbed a handhold and held on tight. In a few moments his discomfort abated. He looked around the pod. He saw chairs, smooth glowing touch-sensitive control services, equipment lockers, and other passengers.

He recognized some of them!

The tall young man with the bronze skin and smooth dome wore a mask, but Talisman knew him from school. The fellow in the sharp black suit was Colin something, but Talisman had known him since first grade. The blonde girl flying the pod – God, she was so smart! – Paris something? Did Ms. Risk go to school with them, too?

But Ms. Risk was talking –

"We need to know," she was saying, "how you obtained the Talisman identity."

Talisman made himself focus.

"He gave it to me," Talisman said, "the original. Right before he died."

"Died?" Ms. Risk said, surprised.

"Yes," Talisman said. "He crumbled to dust right in front of me right after passing an amulet on to me."

She turned to Colin. "Mysteriad?" she asked. "Does that track with what we know about the first Talisman?"

Holy crapballs! Colin from first grade was the Mysteriad?!? Talisman thought.

Colin – Mysteriad! – looked at Talisman, his eyes suddenly seeming deeper and darker than ever they had before.

"He's on the level," Mysteriad said.

Ms. Risk nodded. "Good. We'll bring him in on what's happening this week," she said. "Mysteriad here has detected dark magical energy in Saint Felix in the aftermath of the museum robbery."

Talisman shivered. He thought he could feel Nathan tensing up, next to him.

"Athenian?" Ms. Risk said.

"They stole an artifact during their raid," the tall young man said. His voice boomed even when he spoke quietly. Athenian – like the others, Talisman had read about his exploits and seen them on the news.

"My contacts say it's called the Sword of Cronos," Athenian said. "It may have some mystical properties that our enemies are trying to exploit."

Wow, thought Talisman, *that would totally freak Mrs. Cason out if she knew!*

"G-Girl – our pilot over there," Ms. Risk began.

"Hey, G-Girl," Nathan said, his voice muffled by bandages.

"Hey, Talisman Boy," she said, her voice bright.

Ms. Risk sighed. "Focus, please," she said.

"I've got a lead on the people who attacked the museum on Monday," she said. "They're hiding out somewhere in the warehouse district."

Talisman stood up a little straighter. "What are we waiting for?" he asked. "Let's go round 'em up!"

Ms. Risk held up a hand. "It's not that simple," she said. "We don't know for sure where they are yet. And they have serious hardware at their disposal. If we go in unprepared, we might not make it out alive. And I will not put my team in unnecessary jeopardy if I can help it."

"What about necessary jeopardy?" Talisman asked.

Ms. Risk smiled. It was the most exciting smile Talisman had ever seen.

"Necessary jeopardy is what we're here for," she said.

Talisman gazed at her, his face hidden behind his mask. He felt...dreamy.

"Um...Talisman?" Nathan asked, his voice muffled by the bandages.

He jabbed Talisman in the shoulder.

"Right," Talisman said, "so what do we do now?"

"We stay vigilant for the information we need to move forward," Ms. Risk said. "Are you with us?"

Behind the mask Talisman grinned widely, but he tried to control his voice. "Of course I'm with you," he said. "But what do I need to do?"

G-Girl reached into a pouch on her uniform and pulled out a round device like a small hockey puck. She tossed it and Talisman caught it.

"Communications unit," she said. "We can call you, you can call us."

"Thank you," Talisman said. "Does this make me a member of the Danger Patrol?"

"No," Ms. Risk said. "Let's give this a little time before we talk about membership."

"Do I get one?" Nathan asked.

"Sidekicks don't get one, Talisman Boy," G-Girl said.

"Can I get your number?" Nathan said.

G-Girl spun around in her chair. "Take off the bandages," she said.

"I have to – to protect my secret identity," Nathan said.

"That's what I thought," G-Girl said as she spun back around. But Nathan thought he saw her smile.

"We'll take you back now," Ms. Risk said. "We understand the pressures of civilian life, especially for heroes our age. But stay alert. Trouble could go down at any time."

Chapter Nineteen

The Pod touched down on the museum rooftop, delicately as a hummingbird.

"Faster than a Lyft," G-Girl said. "More powerful than an Uber."

The hatch slid open with a quiet hiss. Talisman took a deep breath, hoping not to puke until the Pod was on its way, and stepped onto the roof. Nathan was right behind him.

Ms. Risk appeared in the hatch behind him, her hand outstretched, holding a thumb drive.

"Take this," she said.

"What's on it?" Talisman asked.

"A few PDFs," Ms. Risk answered. "Hospitals in case you get hurt. Saint Felix police you can turn to for help. Guides to some local tech resources for hero-types like us."

"It's a handbook?" Talisman asked.

"Sort of," she answered. "There's more later if you're approved for membership."

Talisman took the drive from her hand. His fingers brushed her palm as he did so. For a moment he lost his breath but hid it well.

They stood there for a moment.

"I meant what I said," she said. "Be on your toes. There's trouble in the air."

Talisman was quiet.

"We will," Nathan said.

Ms. Risk nodded. "OK," she said. "Well, we'll be going now."

She turned and went back into the pod.

"You're staring," Nathan said.

Talisman shook his head, snapping out of his reverie. "She didn't notice, did she?" he asked.

"That you were ogling her?" Nathan said. "I don't think so."

The Pod door closed. Recessed engines hummed and the Pod took off in a whirl of dust, climbing into the night sky.

"Maybe I have a thing for girls in body armor," Talisman.

"Fickle," Nathan said. "What about that girl the other day? Mallory?"

"Maybe I could chase them both," Talisman said.

"First you have to learn to talk to them," Nathan said.

"He was totally checking you out," Athenian said.

"He's a teenage boy," Ms. Risk said. "I don't know that he can help it. Besides, if he doesn't cut it out, I'll hurt him."

Ms. Risk looked out the windscreen. The lights of Saint Felix twinkled around them. How was it she felt so disconnected from the people but wanted so much to protect the city?

"Nathan was totally hitting on me," G-Girl said.

"Are you sure that was Nathan Saltzman?" Mysteriad asked.

"Duh," said G-Girl. "Did you see that heavy metal t-shirt he had on? Plus, he's Barton's bestie. Of course it was Nathan."

"Problematic," Ms. Risk said. "We all go to Leiter Memorial. Secret identities are still a thing, you know."

"We could alter their memories," G-Girl said. "I could design something. Mysteriad could cast a spell."

Mysteriad shook his head. "No," he said. "I won't mess with their minds like that. Barton didn't ask for this, and he and his friend are just doing the best they can."

"Besides, we don't know for sure what they do and don't know," Athenian added.

Ms. Risk nodded. "We'll play it by ear," she said. "If a problem comes up we'll deal with it."

"What do we do know, boss?" G-Girl asked. "Back to base?"

"Yeah," Ms. Risk said. "Trouble's in the air. I can feel it. We need to rest up for when the storm breaks. Saint Felix is going to need us."

"You didn't tell them the rest," Mysteriad said.

"What's to tell?" she asked. "That Force Majestic is out of the city? That we're the only line of defense right now?"

"Yes," Mysteriad said. "They deserve to know what's at stake."

"Why?" she asked. "Are you concerned they'll freak out? Not come when they're needed?"

"No," he said. "I've known Barton Harper for most of my life. He's a good man. But if something goes down we've got no back up."

"Wrong," she said. She gestured around the Pod. "We're the back up. We're the line."

•   •   •

Barton Harper closed his eyes to sleep and opened them on the infinite beach.

He glanced down the coast to see the temple. He smiled. He liked Spooner. He hoped the man's spirit had some news for him.

He heard a rumble of thunder.

Barton looked out over the clear blue waves. On the horizon he saw a band of ferocious gray storms, storms that glowed with blue-white lightning. He could feel the impending storm as much as see or hear it. He didn't like it. He preferred the way the beach felt before.

"It's part of the cost," Spooner said.

Barton looked to his side. Spooner was there.

"You seem sad," Barton said.

"I am," Spooner said. "Being a super hero is glorious, I ain't gonna lie to you. You see things, go places, feel things regular people don't get to. And it's mighty glorious. But there's that."

Spooner gestured out to the horizon.

"The storm," Barton said.

"That's the cost," Spooner said. "It's coming. I'm sorry for it and I wish I could spare you, kid, but I can't."

Barton stood a little straighter. "I can take it," he said.

Spooner smiled, sad and gentle. "I damn sure hope so," he said.

Chapter Twenty

Ivan Kessler wiped his greasy hands on his already-stained coveralls. He grasped the wrench and sealed the final bolt on the final attack suit. How far past midnight was it? How near the dawn? He didn't know.

He climbed down the ladder, his knees complaining as he did so. He wasn't a young man anymore, as his aging body frequently reminded him.

But he had done it. After decades of research and setbacks, of scorn and derision, of other engineers mocking his ideas – he had done it!

It had taken an alliance with Sparta Eternal, with which he had learned to live. Money and resources made up for a lot. He had been forced to alter his designs to interface with the energies at the command of the detestable Moon.

He hobbled to a work bench. He picked up a mug, sipped from the coffee it contained. It was cold and disgusting, but he needed the boost and drank it anyway.

Sparta Eternal had provided him with the labor needed to complete the half-dozen attack suits in the warehouse now. Each suit was eight feet tall, roughly humanoid in proportion, well armored and armed. They each had an independent power source.

But Moon was to provide their real energy.

He shook his head. The kinds of sorcerous power Moon dealt in was beyond his ken, and he loathed in, on a deep and primal level. But he believed even Moon's sorcery was a form of science, merely something more rational minds had yet to explain.

He looked at his attack suits. They were built to kill, armed with missile racks, machine guns, lasers. It was a shame the ordinary folk of Saint Felix would have to bear the brunt of their assault, but he wouldn't lose any sleep over it.

The woman's body had been drained of its last shred of energy. Her skin was dry, brittle, like a corn husk dried in the field. As the light of the energy transfer faded, she crumbled to dust before Moon's eyes.

Moon was sore, stiff, and tired from conducting the ritual. He wasn't as young as he used to be. He made a mental note to find a ritual to restore some of that youth.

The Scythe hummed with power. He had done his job.

He spoke to his phone, "Call Kessler."

Kessler was looking for a microwave to warm up his disappointing coffee when his phone rang. The screen read "Moon."

He grimaced and answered the phone. "Go for Kessler," he said.

"This is Moon," the other man answered, his voice harsh and whispery. "The ritual is complete. The Scythe of Cronos is charged. Activate the receiver."

"Will do," Kessler said. He placed the phone down. He walked to a computer array on one wall, connected to a dish-shaped antenna, which was in turn connected to the attack suits by thick, insulated cables.

There was no red button, no heavy lever to throw. There was only a command to type, and then Kessler pressed "enter."

He picked his phone back up. "It's done," he said.

Moon didn't answer. He placed his phone down and, holding the Scythe with two hands, raised it to his lips. He whispered an incantation –

- and the Scythe glowed, blinding, green and coruscating –

- and a bolt of power, composed of all the energy and potential of a human life, leapt from the Scythe –

- and seared the dawn sky over Saint Felix –

- and illuminated Kessler's lab like a bomb detonating as it hit the receiver dish. The computer shattered, overloaded, and the

120

cables connected to the attack suits writhed like snakes as the power roared through them.

The suits came to life, with a hum that felt like a scream. Helmet cams activated, lights came on, motors and actuators spun up.

Kessler smiled, then laughed, wild and uncontrollable. He grabbed his phone again, calling General Talin.

The phone rang once, then twice, then Talin entered the room.

Kessler put the phone away. "General Talin!" he said, excitement in his voice. "I was just calling you."

"No need," he said with a quick smile. "The bolt of energy in the sky was quite enough to alert me."

Talin surveyed the gleaming attack suits, unable to hide his pleasure. "Your work…is everything you promised, and more," Talin said. "You will be well paid, I promise."

"Are the pilots prepared?" Kessler asked.

"Yes," Talin said. "They're on their way now. The attack on Saint Felix is about to begin."

Chapter Twenty-One

Barton's clock radio went off. It played a song that was still sort-of new but which he'd already heard too many times. He turned the alarm off and rolled out of bed. He felt refreshed and awake.

Which was weird.

He'd been out late and payed a visit to the...dream temple, or whatever it was called. Was waking up refreshed and awake part of his power set? He kind of liked being a surly teenage in the morning. And it would make his mom suspicious.

He showered, dressed, and rolled into the kitchen for breakfast. He toasted a pop tart and poured a large glass of orange juice and was still working on eating when his mom and little sister entered the kitchen.

His mom just looked at him. "You're awfully...cheerful this morning," she said.

"What can I say? I just woke up on the right side of the bed," Barton said.

She gave him side eye as she prepared her own breakfast.

Lucy got in his face. "Are you on drugs?" she asked.

"No way!" he said with a smile. "I, little sis, am high...on...life!"

She rolled her eyes and poured herself a bowl of cereal.

Barton hopped out of the mini-van in front of Leiter High. He waved as his family drove away.

"See you this afternoon, junkie!" Lucy called.

He heard his mother scolding her as they drove away. Then Nate was there, coffee cup in hand, looking even more disheveled and tired than usual.

"Morning!" Barton called.

Nate winced a little and raised the cup in half-hearted greeting.

"Is it my imagination," Barton said, "or is it even hotter out here than usual?"

"It's not your imagination," Nate said. "Humid, too. Heard on the radio the heat's supposed to break today. Bad storms later."

Barton frowned. "That's a little bit on the nose," he said.

"What? Why?" Nate said.

Barton told him about his dream from the night before.

"Well, that's ominous," Nate said.

"We know something terrible is going on," Barton. "Is today the day? Does everything go sideways today?"

Nate just shook his head. "I don't know," he said. 'But your better be on your toes."

They made their way into school to Mrs. Cason's class. Barton grinned at Nate.

"Be prepared for anything, Talisman Boy," Barton said.

Nate's expression grew more sour. "You better hope I never get powers of my own," he said. "Or I will beat your ass."

Barton went about his day. Even in the air-conditioned halls of his high school, the heat grew more intense, the air heavier with humidity.

Was it his imagination, this sense of dread? Or was the ghost of Spooner all too correct?

He was headed to gym around noon when the building shook.

Dust fell from the ceiling tiles. Barton looked at the other students around him and saw shock and surprise on their faces.

The building shook again.

Someone screamed. Students began to scatter. Barton heard swearing and the beginnings of panic.

He looked around. He had to get to a window, try to see something.

Barton pushed his way through crowds of milling, frightened students. Someone was speaking over the intercom, but Barton couldn't tell who it was. He made his way to an outside wall and a window and looked outside.

Clouds were gathering. He thought he saw a flash of lightning and heard a rumble of thunder but they were too far away to have affected the school.

He pulled out his phone and quickly looked up a local TV news outlet. They showed grainy, shaky footage of something in metro Saint Felix.

Barton saw…armored suits? Bolts of energy flying from outstretched mechanical hands?

Then he saw on the video feed a car hit by one of those energy bolts explode.

For a moment, he was stunned.

Someone just died, he thought.

A tear ran down his face. Then another. Then he began to sob.

Someone died, he thought. *Someone died. I wasn't there. I couldn't help.*

His breath was coming in ragged gasps now.

He leaned against the cinderblock wall. It was cool and smooth to the touch.

126

Then she was there, her hand on his shoulder.

"Mallory?" Barton said. "Mallory Savage?"

"Barton," she said, urgently but gently, "I'm glad I found you. It's time."

He didn't understand. "Time for what?" he asked.

"Time to stand," she said, "Talisman."

He began to speak. "What do you – "

And then it hit him like a ton of bricks.

"You," he said. "You're *her*."

She nodded. Her smile was surprisingly kind.

"It's terrible," she said. "It's a nightmare. And we stand between it and the city."

Barton wiped his hand across his face. He stood up, straight and tall.

"What now?" he asked.

"The Pod is on the way," she said. "When it gets here we get on board. Then we go downtown and fight."

Chapter Twenty-Two

Leiter Memorial shook as Barton and Mal darted through the halls. Students ran, crying out in fear. Teachers attempted to corral their charges into the relative safety of classrooms. Barton heard someone on the intercom trying to restore order, but he couldn't tell who it was. Principal Fleming, maybe?

"We're not that close to downtown," Mal said over the din. She didn't scream, seemed hardly to raise her voice. She had a way of cutting through noise. "Whatever's going on, it must be horrendously powerful."

Barton shook his head. "Then let Force Majestic handle it!" he said.

Mal stopped and pulled him into an empty corner in the hallway. "They're out of town," she said. "Danger Patrol is it, it's all Saint Felix has."

Barton looked at her for a moment, flabbergasted.

"Well," he said, attempting to be glib, "who wants to live forever, anyway?"

"I do," she said. "Look, I'll die to save lives if I have to."

She grinned, a little wild.

"But it's not ever plan A," she said. "Now, come on!"

They took off again. "Where are we going?" Barton asked.

"Like I said, the Pod is on its way," she answered.

"How are we gonna do this without losing out secret identities?" Barton asked.

"You're gonna love this," Mal said.

They emerged from the front of the building and made their way to the car rider line. No one was there, and no cars were in line.

"Are you…are you one of those superheroes that's, you know, crazy?" Barton asked.

"Not at all," Mal said.

Three people came out of the building after them: tall, handsome Tucker Alexander, with his smooth dome, Colin Ballard in his rumpled jeans and t-shirt, and preppy Paris Paxton, nose in her phone.

Barton's jaw dropped. "Holy crap," he said.

"Yeah," Mal said. "It's us."

Tucker and Colin and Paris took a look at Barton.

"So," Colin said, "it's all out in the open with this guy?"

"Yep," Mal said. "The poop has hit the fan, Colin, and we have to trust him. The city is in danger."

Colin considered for a moment, and then stuck his hand out to Barton. "Welcome aboard, Barton."

Barton shook Colin's hand. "Thank you," he said.

"There'll be training later," Tucker said. "For now, just watch yourself, and be careful out there. We don't know what's going on yet."

Paris stepped up to the edge of the sidewalk, still on her phone. In a few moments, a rusty, dented, dirty mini-van appeared in the lane, cruising around to come to a stop in front of them. The door slid open.

"Get in!" Paris said. She stepped inside, followed by Mal, then Tucker and Colin.

Barton shook his head, and then stepped inside as well. Then he received his next shock, as he realized he was inside the Pod.

"Aha!" he said, as the Pod began to move, heading out along the car rider lane. "The Pod has a cloak!"

Paris turned from the pilot's chair to smile at him. "Just one," she said. "The only mode I've gotten to work so far is the mini-van, but that's OK because that's the one we needed today."

"Are we out of visual range of the school?" Mal asked.

"Yes, boss," Paris said.

"Good," Mal said. "Disengage cloak and take us up."

Barton felt a surge of power through the ship as it leapt into the sky.

"Set course for HQ," Mal said. Paris nodded.

Tucker took a seat at a console and began entering something on a keyboard. Monitors mounted on the Pod's interior hull flickered to life. They showed a variety of video feeds: local news, traffic cameras, videos playing on social media, and what Barton thought was drone footage.

The monitors revealed the attack on the city. People in some kind of mechanical war suits struck throughout the downtown area. Barton thought he could see missiles fired from shoulder-mounted launchers, machine gun bursts from arm-mounted cannons, and over-powered mechanical arms heaving objects – and people! – through the air.

"Comms are up and running," Tucker said. "I'm running them through the Force Majestic database. No identity on them yet. And they haven't identified themselves or made any demands yet."

Mal looked at the video closely. "Those mech suits are way overpowered for their size," she said. "Colin, could this be connected the mystical forces you've sensed this week? Could they be the source of this power?"

Colin thought for a moment. "I'd bet on it," he said.

Mal turned to Barton. "We're headed to our HQ," she said. "We need our uniforms and out gear. How do you suit up?"

Barton reached into his shirt and touched the medallion. He closed his eyes, focused...

"Wow," Colin said.

Barton opened his eyes as the Talisman.

"In all fairness," Mal said, "that is pretty cool."

Chapter Twenty-Three

General Talin rode in the great black SUV. He scanned the battlefield with binoculars, switching back and forth between them and reports from his people coming in on his phone.

Phase I was quite simple: destruction.

The war suits, all half-dozen of them, inflicted magnificent damage on Saint Felix. Kessler's technology and Moon's dark magic combined to create something truly terrifying.

An arc of electricity from one suit detonated the gas tank of a car.

A missile from another suit arced into a store front, exploding in searing orange flame.

A blast of machine gun fire sent a group of panicked pedestrians fleeing.

Saint Felix Police were on site, in full riot gear, doing their best at crowd control, but failing against the power of the suits.

He couldn't help smiling. The results of their efforts spoke for themselves.

Talin turned to his driver. "Head for the secondary location," he said, and the driver responded. They drove aggressively through the increasingly crazier traffic.

Phase II was out of his hands but should begin any time now.

He expected Force Majestic to show up any time. The war suits would crush the ridiculous costumed heroes, and then…

…then, there would be Phase III.

•   •   •

Talisman looked around at the Danger Patrol's headquarters. They had been there less than five minutes, but already his friends were suited up and preparing for battle. Information poured from the monitors than ringed the room. Attackers in war suits were wreaking havoc in downtown Saint Felix. Local news as well as local, state, and federal emergency channels had yet to report on the identity of the attackers, but so far casualties had been miraculously low.

That was bound to change.

"No demands have been issued yet," Ms. Risk said. "And we have no ID on the attackers, either."

Athenian shook his head. "How is that possible?" he said. "How can we not know an outfit with this kind of tech and resources?"

"This must be their first big move," Ms. Risk said. "A group who's been lurking in the shadows for a long time, people finally ready to level up."

"But why here?" Athenian asked. "And why now?"

Ms. Risk was quiet as she thought. But Talisman spoke up first.

"They picked Saint Felix for Force Majestic," Talisman said. "They're expecting the big-time super team to show up. And they picked now...

"...because they're finally ready for them," he finished.

Talisman felt a chill in the room.

"He's right," Ms. Risk finally said. "But we've got no choice if we want to help."

G-Girl entered the room, wiping grease from her hands on her red coveralls.

"G=Girl, is the Pod ready?" Ms. Risk asked.

"The shield generators are installed," G-Girl said. "But they may not work. Untested, prototype, blah blah blah, keep your fingers crossed."

Ms. Risk nodded. "Mysteriad, what can you tell me?"

Mysteriad hovered, cross-legged, in a corner, a faint sense of electricity in the air around him. He opened his eyes when Ms. Risk spoke to him, but Talisman had the sense he was seeing a world altogether different from the one they shared.

"Those suits take power from somewhere else," he said, a weird bass tone to his voice. "I can find it. I can stop it. But I must go...alone."

And in a shimmer of mist and a smell like a thunderstorm, he was gone.

"Does he do that a lot?" Talisman asked.

"More than we would like," Ms. Risk said.

"But on the other hand, I'm pretty sure he goes places we'd rather not ourselves – literally and metaphorically," G-Girl said.

"We've been here too long already. Time to load up," Ms. Risk said. "We're got intel and we've augmented the Pod. Athenian, G-Girl, Talisman, to the Pod."

"I'm scared to death," Talisman said.

"You don't have to come," Athenian said. "You're brand new to this life. We would think no less of you."

"I would think less of me," Talisman said, smiling ruefully behind his golden mask. "Just make sure to tell my family I loved them if I don't come back."

"That's the spirit!" G-Girl said as they moved to the rooftop.

The Pod sat there, humming with power, and they climbed aboard. In an instant G-Girl had the hatch sealed and the Pod in the air. Talisman took a seat, strapped himself in. He could see Ms. Risk and Athenian scanning incoming data on the downtown attackers. "Can you see a weakness?" Ms. Risk asked. "Is there some flaw in those suits I'm missing?"

Athenian stayed silent.

Chapter Twenty-Four

G-Girl brought the Pod over the rubble-strewn battlefield at the heart of Saint Felix. The monitors inside the craft displayed images and information that looked like video from a warzone. The attacking war suits fired machine guns, missiles, arcs of electricity, and more.

Talisman was looking at a monitor when one of the war suits suddenly looked back.

"Guys," he said.

"I see it!" G-Girl

"Where is Force Majestic, again?" Talisman asked.

"The moon, I think," G-Girl said.

"Nothing for it then, I guess," Talisman said. He unstrapped from his seat and walked to the hatch. He stumbled a bit as the Pod banked but caught himself on the bulkhead.

"What are you doing?" Ms. Risk shouted.

"My job, I guess," Talisman shrugged. He hit a switch that opened the hatch.

He took a deep breath and a running start and leapt from the Pod.

"He's got guts, I'll give him that," G-Girl said.

"A lot of good that'll do us if he gets himself killed!" Ms. Risk said.

·　　　　·　　　　·

Talisman plummeted the three stories from the pod to the pavement. He felt a surge of panic but choked it back, and then made a dramatic landing as his feet and fists crunched concrete.

"Superhero landing!" he said. "Yes!"

Then he looked up.

He was staring directly at one of the war suits.

It loomed over him, all steel plate and bristling armaments. He scanned it as quickly as he could, looking it over for a weak point he could attack.

He couldn't find one.

And then a mounted turret on the thing swiveled and pointed straight at him.

He swore loudly and leapt to his right as the turret opened up with a burst of gunfire that turned the sidewalk he'd been standing on into fine gravel.

Talisman looked around, pushing through fear, fighting to keep a clear head.

There!

He spotted a hunk of masonry, something the size of a washing machine, blasted from a nearby building.

How strong am I? he wondered. He dashed to the fallen masonry and wrapped his arms around it.

He heard the whine of a motor as the turret tracked him. He had only seconds.

He heaved, feeling muscles in his arms and legs and back strain with the effort, but he picked the masonry up from the ground. Then, with a supreme effort, he hurled it towards the warsuit!

And with a crunch of crumbling concrete and a whine of damaged machinery, he found his target!

The war suit staggered, hydraulic fluid spurting from damaged systems, sparks flying from shredded electronics.

Talisman pumped his fist.

Then, as Talisman watched, the war suit straightened itself. Cracked and broken armor seemed to heal before his eyes. Electronic systems repaired themselves, becoming whole as he watched.

"That's impossible," he said, knowing the truth of his eyes as he watched.

Then the turret pointed at him again.

The Pod circled the block above Talisman's battle. Its cameras and sensors were trained on the confrontation, and its crew watched intently as the battle raged.

"No," Ms. Risk said as she watched. "It can't be!"

The war suit had repaired itself as they watched and was again bearing down on Talisman.

"What could be causing that?" Ms. Risk asked.

G-Girl shook her head in astonishment. 'I – I don't know," she stammered. "Even the most advanced nanotech we know of is still years away from anything on that scale, even in the lab!"

Athenian looked at a set of readings on a viewscreen. "None of this makes sense," he said gravely. "And you both know what that means."

Ms. Risk and G-Girl traded a look. "Yeah," G-Girl said. "It means magic."

"Those suits are being augmented with dark magic," Athenian said. "That's what Mysteriad sensed. That's what he took off to go fight."

144

A heavy silence hung inside the pod as the sounds of war raged outside.

"What do we do?" G-Girl asked in a whisper.

Ms. Risk was quiet. G-Girl took her hand.

"Mal, sweetie," she said. "what do we do?"

Something changed in Ms. Risk's eyes.

"We buy Mysteriad time," she said. "And we help the new guy down their kick some butt."

G-Girl smiled. "Bringing weapons on line," she said.

"Weapons?" Ms. Risk asked. "Our mentors were very clear this ship shouldn't have weapons!"

The engines whined as the Pod angled down. "Do you always do what you're told?" G-Girl asked.

Ms. Risk smiled, something wolf-like and dangerous. "No," she said. "I don't. Take us in!"

Chapter Twenty-Five

Mysteriad materialized. Instantly, he crouched, senses attuned to his surroundings.

He felt cold wash over him, through him. A mist clung to the floor. His gaze pierced the gloom to see walls of rough stone with rusted chains and unused sconces. He could smell something…rotting, somewhere nearby. A steady drip…drip…drip of water echoed in the hallways.

As for his other senses, the ones for other levels of reality, they burned with knowledge, too.

Mysteriad stood and straightened his suit coat. He walked forward, mist parting around his feet.

Then he saw it. The Scythe of Cronos. The artifact stolen from the museum! It hung in mid-air, with sizzling white fire pulsing around it.

That's the answer, he thought. *I can feel it!*

"I can sense you," he said. "I can sense the power flowing through this place."

Then the man stood before him, as if from nowhere. He had a pale face, with slicked back black hair, and wore a white shirt with rolled-up sleeves and khakis.

"You're Miles Moon," Mysteriad said.

"My reputation precedes me," Moon said.

Mysteriad looked at the tattoos up and down Moon's arms. "Nice ink," he said. "My Dad says I'm too young."

"Yes, your Dad…how is old Bailey, anyway?" Moon asked.

"…indisposed," said Mysteriad, straining to keep the shock from his face.

"Oh, yes," Moon said. "I know your father. And out of respect, I won't kill you."

Then Moon's hands were wreathed in eldritch red fire.

"Of course, there are worse fates than death," Moon said.

Mysteriad raised his hands. He mouthed a word and a blue shield crackled into being in front of him.

"I'll have to talk to dad later," Mysteriad said. "And tell him how I kicked your – "

Dagmara drove the SUV into the townhouse's garage. She used the remote and lowered the door behind her. The house wasn't close to the battle, but dust still fell from the ceiling from the shock

She had just stepped out to get some groceries and all hell had broken loose.

Leaving her purchases in the vehicle, she bolted from the driver's seat and into her home. She took the stairs three at a time until she reached the door to the Patrol's HQ on the top level. She burst through, knowing before she did so that she would find the place empty.

Fear gripped her heart. She loved Mal like a daughter, would protect her all she could, but they had both chosen their paths long ago. She knew where Mal – where Ms. Risk would be without having to look.

But look she did, at the monitors ringing the room. There was the new Talisman, gold and gleaming, standing against some kind of war suit. And there was the Pod, G-Girl's pride and joy.

And there, hanging out the hatch, was Ms. Risk. She wielded some kind of energy weapon.

Dagmara's fear turned to irritation. The younger generation was prohibited from using weapons like that! Where did they get that?

G-Girl probably built it. As brilliant as she was it probably only took a few hours. She was going to tear that girl a new –

April Harper swore as her coffee spilled across her desk.

Her building shook. *What's going on?* she wondered.

The building shook again, harder. She could feel her heart start to race.

She stood from her desk and raced to a window. Others from her office did the same. A murmur of conversation quickly changed to panicked cries of fear as they saw what was going on.

A pitched battle was raging in the streets of Saint Felix, just outside their building!

April looked downwards the many stories to the ground. She could see – what was that? Some kind of robot? No, it was someone in some kind of war suit –

Good God! she thought, as she saw a hot orange sheet of flame explode from the arm of the battle suit. The flame washed over a figure –

It was a super hero! April didn't recognize the hero – he wore some kind of gold uniform – in a flash he'd dodged the flame and then turned around to deal a blow to the war suit, a blow so devasting that she could hear its echo even through the glass.

Then she saw the weird little hovercraft, with a woman in costume hanging out the side, firing some kind of laser blast at the war suit below.

She pumped her fist. "Blast 'em!" she cried, though she knew full well they couldn't hear her.

The laser had no effect April could see.

She watched the golden hero dodge and battle as best he could. She felt an inexplicable stab of fear as she watched. Who was this person? Who was risking everything for the innocent people of Saint Felix?

Then the building shook again, and she knew she had to get out.

Ms. Risk swung back into the Pod.

"G-Girl," she said. "Take us up!"

"You got it, boss!" G-Girl cried.

Ms. Risk grabbed the leather strap by the door. She hung on tight as the Pod swooped over the rooftops.

"What have you got in mind?" G-Girl asked.

"I've got a hunch to play!" Ms. Risk shouted over the din. "No time to explain! Wish me luck!"

And she leapt from the pod to the building below.

Athenian shook his head. "I hate it when she does that," he said.

Chapter Twenty-Six

OWWW that's HOT –

Talisman felt the flames wash over him, knew with uncommon certainty that he was going to die, and then felt a great flood of relief as he realized he was in fact still alive.

He spared a moment to look himself over. The fire hadn't injured him.

Chalk up another level of resistance, he thought.

Then he leapt back at the warsuit, pummeling it with all his might.

G-Girl dodged a news helicopter maneuvering too close to the battle. She swore loudly. "This is getting out of hand," she said.

Her hand hovered over a panel on her control board. She gave it a moment's consideration more, then activated the touch screen interface.

A head's up holographic targeting reticle sprang into life over the cockpit. Athenian's jaw dropped.

"G-Girl," he said, his voice wary. "Is that a targeting system?"

"Yep!" she said, voice cheery. "It's for the particle beam."

"Particle beam?" Athenian said as the Pod banked for another pass at the warsuit Talisman battled. "Force Majestic forbade us from having weapons on the Pod!"

"Yeah, well," she said, "if we live through this I'll take the heat."

She handed Athenian a small headset. "Get on this and tell Talisman to get out of the way, please and thank you."

•   •   •

Talisman slammed his golden fists into the warsuit's leg again and again. It swatted at him, and only his enhanced speed allowed to dodge. He knew he could take a punch, and had already taken several, but could feel his strength beginning to ebb.

And the blasted thing hadn't shown any sign of even slowing down!

Then he saw the Pod bank in a short fast arc back towards him and the warsuit. Athenian's voice burst from the Pod's speakers. "Talisman!" Athenian said. "Get clear!"

Talisman didn't need to be told twice. He put on a burst of speed and rolled behind a pile of rubble.

He peered from behind cover to watch what happened next.

A glittering white beam lanced from the Pod almost faster than he could perceive to strike the warsuit. It struck something – perhaps the fuel for the flame thrower – and the war suit exploded in a ball of oily orange flame.

Talisman pumped his fist. "Yes!" he shouted. He immediately felt guilty – someone in that suit was probably burning, he had no business cheering death, no matter how well deserved.

The war suit burned brightly. But then things got....

....weird.

The fire went out. Talisman could see blackened metal plates, ruptured hydraulic lines, and sparking electronics. And before his eyes...

...they reassembled.

Like time lapse photography of a wound healing the war suit reassembled in front of him.

"No!" Talisman hissed. "That's impossible!"

Then it all made sense. It hit his mind all at once. The theft of the artifact. Its supernatural properties. The dark magic Mysteriad sensed.

The war suits weren't just technological.

They healed themselves through magic.

They were unstoppable.

"Oh, crap," Talisman said as the flame thrower turned back at him.

"Oh, crap," G-Girl said.

"I didn't just see that," Athenian said. "Did I?"

G-Girl scanned the screens in front of her. "Another warsuit is on this block," she said.

Before Athenian could say anything, she maneuvered the Pod in a hard-left bank. Alarms screamed in the confined space and warning lights went off like the lights in a dance club.

Athenian heard the wash of a missile's exhaust outside the hull.

"Air to air missile!" G-Girl gasped out. "Hold on! it's coming back around!"

G-Girl had her hands full flying. Athenian grabbed the control console and pulled himself to the particle beam controls. Straining hard against the g-forces of their flight, moving and thinking as fast as he could, he targeted the missile.

Somewhere a target lock warning screamed at him. He put it out of his mind.

Only seconds – no, it was mere instants now –

The reticle aligned with the missile.

Athenian pressed the button.

The particle beam closed the distance to the missile in an instant.

It detonated, the explosion blinding white.

Athenian grinned wildly, even as the Pod rocked from the explosion's shockwave.

Alarms kept blaring. "What's wrong?" he cried over them.

"Second shot killed the generator," G-Girl said, her voice frantic. "I've got just enough power to bring us down!"

Athenian held on tighter. The Pod shock around them.

Then it plowed into the road. Shattered concrete and car parts flew into the air around them.

Athenian heard G-Girl cry out.

Then they were still.

Athenian was at the hatch. "We have to go," he said. "We're now officially a sitting duck."

G-Girl winced as she unbuckled. Athenian thought she looked like someone leaving behind their child. Then she was with him and they were through the hatch.

Chapter Twenty-Seven

Mysteriad dodged a glittering spike of indigo energy. He slammed into the stone wall. He gasped in pain, before quickly reorienting himself. He moved again just before another spike would have impaled him. Moon threw spell after spell at him, pushing Mysteriad to his limit and far beyond.

He ran, panting for breath, mind racing, magic hanging like electricity in the air around him. He gestured with his left hand and murmured an incantation and a half-dome of golden light formed around him, changing position as it blocked bolts of energy.

He still shuddered as those bolts struck the shield. The most powerful spells Mysteriad knew were - and he hated this thought – like child's play before Moon.

"Give up, my son," Moon said. His voice echoed. "I can make your death…ordinary. Quick. Mostly painless."

Mysteriad smirked. Yeah, like he was just gonna quit.

Ms. Risk leapt from rooftop to rooftop. She had made a guess – that whoever was in charge of these war suits was in the area. There was something about the tactics they used, something she couldn't put her finger on, that made her think if she was lucky, she might be able to tag their leader in the field.

She felt a knife of guilt. She had left her team to battle the warsuits without her. But in the end she was only human, a fighter in armor. There was a limit to how much she could do toe-to-toe with those things.

She saw something: a black SUV. It wasn't fleeing the scene.

That by itself was strange. But as she watched the SUV through the telescopic lenses in her cowl, she saw that the SUV was more-or-less orbiting the field of battle.

She made her way towards it.

The warsuits had exceeded Talon's expectations. The damage they wrought, their mystical ability to heal themselves, the fear they caused...

Good. Time to make his move.

"Take me to WFLX," he said. "I think they'll want to speak with me."

Ms. Risk felt the wind in her hair as she clung to the top of the tractor trailer. She'd jumped from truck to truck as she tailed the SUV through the city.

Now the SUV had come to a stop. She rolled from the top of the truck and landed lightly on the pavement.

Ms. Risk looked up. She and the SUV were outside WFLX, a local TV station.

Uh-oh, she thought. *Probably time for a manifesto.*

She manipulated her cowl's touch controls and brought the local broadcast into focus inside one of the lenses.

She carefully approached the front door of the station as she watched the broadcast. She saw no guards yet.

On the TV signal, a man she didn't recognize sat behind the anchor desk. He'd already started speaking.

"Hello, Saint Felix," he said. "My name is General Nicholas Talin."

Talin sat before the cameras. His men guarded the studio. Others kept their weapons pointed at the cameramen.

"I have come to Saint Felix to begin a revolution," he said. "More than that, to begin the next chapter of human history. Too long have the strong been in service of the weak. If you search your hearts, you know the truth: that the strong are meant to lead, to explore, to win the future by the strength of their will."

He took a breath. He'd waited so long for this chance.

"My organization is called Sparta Eternal. And we seek to weed out the weak, to deliver the strong to freedom. Even now our warriors have begun the cleansing. The weak who cannot stand the attack will perish.

"From here, we will expand our vision to the rest of the country, and then the world."

He took a breath. "You have a choice to make. Are you the weak, or are you the strong?"

Ms. Risk crept silently through the station, avoiding guards, even as she watched Talin rise from his chair and approach the camera. His intense blue eyes flashed. She could feel his charisma.

"Join us. Step up. Prove your strength. You have no need to hide in your homes if you are strong enough. Do it – do it now."

Oh no, Ms. Risk thought.

"Take to the streets. Rise up. If you want to join us, find the weak...

"And kill them."

Chapter Twenty-Eight

Nathan hunkered down in the library of Leiter High with a group of other students. He didn't know any of them, but it was better than being alone.

The battle with the war suits was close enough to shake the building. Every student who had a phone was watching live video of the battle.

Nathan knew his dad would be trying to figure out how to safely get him out of the building. But he also knew roads would be closed, cops would be out, and the National Guard was probably already on the way.

Then he heard the words from the guy on the news, the guy who said he was responsible for all of this. Something about killing the weak.

He exchanged a look with the kids he was with.

"Just who are you guys?" he asked.

"We're the Chess Club," a redhaired girl was glasses answered.

The doors to the library burst open. A pair of boys entered, each one approaching six feet in height.

"We're here for the weak," they said.

"Ah, crap," Nathan said.

Ms. Risk ran through the TV station. All thoughts of stealth cast aside, she made her way to the control booth. She had to stop the broadcast.

He's going to get innocent people killed, she thought. *All some people need is the reason to kill, and he's giving it to them!*

A pair of guards in matching uniforms stood outside the booth. She had only seconds. Seconds…

…and her lifetime of training.

Before they could raise their rifles she had leapt into the air, planting a kick on the wall. She led with her other foot, her bootheel smashing into the faces of each guard in turn.

She landed lightly on the floor at the same instant the unconscious bodies of the guards smashed down. She allowed herself one quick self-satisfied smile before shoving open the door.

Her face fell.

Talin was already there.

He had a pistol pointed at the head of one of the technicians.

"How did you get in here so fast?" Ms. Risk demanded.

"Does it matter?" Talin asked.

She took in the room. Technicians hunkered over their consoles, frightened for the lives. Another kept a shoulder-mounted camera pointed at Talin. She could see his face on the screen. The signal was still going on.

"This world has been run for the benefit of the weak for too long," Talin said. The technician with the gun to her head was clearly terrified. Ms. Risk looked for an opening but couldn't see one.

"We've come here to make a point," Talin said. She couldn't tell if he was speaking to her or the camera or both. "And we're going to make it. The world doesn't have to be this way. We can rise up and change it!"

The situation was falling apart in front of her. She had to do something. Stop Talin, save the hostage –

-but how?

Nathan jumped to his feet. He stepped between the Chess Club –

- Chess Club, why did it have to be the Chess Club? –

- and the two six footers that had entered the library.

"If you're after the weak," he said, "you're gonna have to go through me first."

Somewhere behind him, he heard the Chess Club take exception to this. "Just try me, buster!" someone complained.

The two large students looked at Nathan. In response he took a martial arts stance – something he'd seen in a movie, sure, but it was what he had.

The two newcomers laughed.

"Do you think we're here to kill the chess club?" one of them said.

"We're here to keep them safe," the other said.

One of them looked around. He spotted an empty bookcase. He hefted it over one shoulder and moved it to block the library entrance.

He turned to Nathan. "I don't know if anyone at our school is gonna listen to that guy or not," he said. "But there's no way I let some boomer buttwipe kill people here."

Nathan smiled. "Can I help?" he said.

Mysteriad could hear his own heartbeat. It was slowing. His breathing was slowing. Or was time slowing around him? Was he running out of time?

Mystical energy crackled around him. Moon wore him down, more and more. He'd be dead soon. Would he see his father again?

His skin tingled. The magic in the air, he thought.

Maybe...maybe he had one last spell in him. He could barely focus, so it had to be something simple.

Simple...but powerful.

Fortunately for Mysteriad, Moon was sloppy. He'd used attacks that left the air thick with residual magic energy.

Mysteriad closed his eyes. He envisioned the Scythe nearby. He could visualize the magic – he pictured it, in his mind's eye, as he whispered words from a language long dead –

And magic wove into a needle. A small needle, of glowing power, that Mysteriad sent through the air –

- and into the Scythe.

Moon snapped his head around. "No!" he hissed.

And the Scythe shattered.

The air swirled around them, and Mysteriad heard a peal of thunder from another realm entirely.

The magic in the air thrummed, and something shifted, and ectoplasm, green and gooey, splashed to the floor. Mysteriad was covered in it, as was Moon.

Mysteriad sat up, slightly disgusted to see the state of his suit. Moon looked at him, enraged. With a wordless snarl, Moon charged him.

And with a flash of energy, a whirling portal opened in the air, just behind him!

A thick black tentacle lashed out, wrapping itself around Moon's waist. Moon writhed uselessly against the grip of the thing, screaming as he was pulled relentlessly into the portal.

As it began to close, Mysteriad thought he saw –

Yes!

His dad!

A gray, translucent vision, but smiling.

"Someone on this side would like a word with Moon," Bailey Ballard said.

Mysteriad smiled.

"You did good, son," Bailey said. "See you soon."

And then the image of his father, and the portal, were gone.

Mysteriad, slightly shaky, managed to stand. He brushed ectoplasm from his lapel.

"I wonder if I can find a spell for dry cleaning," he said to himself.

Chapter Twenty-Nine

Talisman could feel his strength ebbing.

He charged in front of the fleeing pedestrians – he didn't even have time to see who they were - and took a blast of electricity to his chest from an attacking warsuit.

The people he had protected scattered into the rubble and confusion. Talisman heard screams as they went, and was that – did someone say thank you?

That's nice, he thought as he lay in the street. *Considerate.*

He'd felt that last blast, felt his heart skip a beat. There was an upper limit to how much punishment he could take in this form, and he was rapidly getting there.

I don't want to die, he thought.

Talisman staggered to his feet.

I could run. Switch back to good old Barton Harper. No one would ever know.

Well, Nathan would know. But he'd forgive me.

He looked around. He saw Athenian, masked face, smooth head gleaming, throw a piece of broken girder at a warsuit. The warsuit slammed the girder aside and then fired a machine gun burst at Athenian, who just barely dodged.

I'd know. I'd know that I ran. I'd know that I had it in me to save even one more innocent life and that I'd ran.

G-Girl dodged from one pile of rubble to the next, seeking cover as best she could, firing a weapon of some kind – some kind of blue energy blast. Her target took the blast, energy sparking, and then, before his eyes, repaired itself.

***I'd** know.*

He cracked his knuckles, brushed some dirt from his leg, and looked around.

He saw a piece of debris – from a car, maybe – about the size of a mail box. He walked over, wrapped his arms around it, and hefted it up.

His knees threatened to buckle, but he kept standing. He looked around for the nearest warsuit. Spotting it, he hurled the debris through the air with all his strength.

With a crash of grinding metal, his aim true, the warsuit crashed to the sidewalk under the hunk of metal. Systems sparked and hydraulic fluid spurted into the air.

"YES!" Talisman cried, a hot rush of triumph running through his veins.

It began to rise, weapons aimed at him.

He smirked, still standing, unbowed. He thought of his sister and his mother and his friends, and braced himself.

Then something new happened.

A flash of - what was that? Blue fire? from the downed warsuit.

And then it didn't repair itself.

The warsuit lurched to its feet, still sparking, still damaged. Talisman thought he could hear gears grinding, relays clicking and misfiring.

Huh. So that's what hope feels like, he thought

He ran, fresh energy coursing through him. He leapt from the street to a broken bus, and jumped from it, launching himself feet first through the air at the warsuit.

He slammed into it, the suit tumbling over backwards as Talisman flipped through the air, then landing.

Behind him, a hatch opened. Someone in a helmet and fatigues climbed out of the war suit. Talisman raced to the suit.

"Warsuit Zero-1 to Talin," the pilot said into a helmet microphone. "Warsuit Zero-1 to Talin!"

The pilot's cries became more desperate as he saw Talisman approaching, and then they stopped altogether as Talisman slugged him in the jaw.

The pilot dropped like a rock.

G-Girl suddenly appeared at Talisman's side.

"What do you think happened?" Talisman asked.

"If I had to guess," she said, "I'd say there was some mystical side to this that Mysteriad has sorted out."

They heard a crunching sound, and then looked around to see Athenian on the back of a warsuit ripping great hunks of machinery and electronics out.

Talisman nodded to G-Girl. "Off hand, I'd say you're right," he said.

Then a fresh surge of energy ran through him.

"Are you ready to finish this?" he asked.

She slapped a fresh power pack into her energy weapon.

"Let's," she said.

Talin glanced from the camera to the TV monitors in the control room. He saw the young heroes battling his warsuits.

Something had gone wrong!

They were taking the war suits apart!

He heard desperate cries from his pilots over his earpiece. His blood ran cold – this wasn't supposed to happen, this was impossible, the suits were invulnerable –

"No!" he whispered under his breath. Then, shouting, "No!"

His hostage, sensing a chance, stomped down on Talin's foot with all her might. Talin felt it, even through the heavy boot.

He'd lost control of the situation, he needed to get it back –

- but then there was the girl and her fist was flying through the air right at him –

- and he was out before he hit the floor.

Chapter Thirty

Talisman sat on the ledge on top of the building across from police headquarters. He'd been there since before sunset, watching the Saint. Felix cops bring in the members of Sparta Eternal.

"Maybe not so Eternal, after all," he said.

He felt confused. They'd won, beaten the bad guys, saved the city. He expected to feel some kind of triumph. But instead, he just felt tired, sore, and more than a little sad.

One by one, his new allies – new friends? – joined him. Ms. Risk landed lightly nearby, silent as a ninja. Mysteriad appeared in a puff of smoke. G-Girl and Athenian climbed up the fire escape from the street below. They each had a grin on their sweat-covered, grimy faces, except Mysteriad, who appeared clean and peaceful.

"I'm sorry about the Pod," Talisman said.

"It's OK," G-Girl said. "Cost of doing business. It just gives me an excuse to build the next one."

"So. Dirty, bruised, bloody," Ms. Risk said, "but we're all alive. And the bad guys are going to jail."

Talisman heard sirens in the distance, ambulances and firetrucks. "Not enough people are still alive," he said.

Ms. Risk put her hand on his shoulder. "We can't save everybody," she said. "As hard as we try."

Athenian sat down beside him. "I know how you feel," he said, his deep voice surprisingly soft. "But you have to remind yourself, every day, of the good we accomplish. Many more people will see the dawn tomorrow because of us."

Talisman nodded. "I guess that has to be enough, doesn't it," he said.

They were quiet for a moment. A paddy wagon pulled up and cops escorted a handcuffed General Talin into the building. He struggled against them, reluctant, defiant in defeat. But they got him inside.

"I won't miss that guy," Talisman said.

"Be careful what you say," Athenian said. "These guys have a habit of coming back for more."

"Then why do it?" Talisman said. "Is there a point?"

"Of course there's a point," Mysteriad said. "You do understand evil is real, right? Not just people making bad choices. Real, tangible, evil. And we stand against it."

Talisman was quiet again.

"Do you intend to keep doing this?" G-Girl asked.

Talisman paused for a moment. "Yeah," he said. "Yeah, I do."

The four other teenagers traded looks between them, each nodded. Ms. Risk turned to him. "Then, if you want, you're one of us. One of the Danger Patrol."

"You can train with us, fight with us, share our resources," G-Girl said.

"We can help you cope with the things you see in this line of work," Mysteriad said. "Sometimes it can be...haunting."

"And sometimes it can be incredible," Athenian said. "Sometimes we get to go places and see things we could never have seen outside this life."

"Can you help me with my Mom?" Talisman said. "I don't know how I'm going to explain getting home late in all this, much less how I'm a superhero."

"We're all legacies," G-Girl said. "Our families fought the good fight before we were even born. So, I guess I don't really know how I'd tell your mom."

"Experience would suggest...maybe giving it a little time," Ms. Risk said. "You kind of got thrown in the deep end here. Honestly, you're lucky you got out OK."

"Take some time," Athenian said. "Train. Study. Learn more about who and what you are now."

Talisman thought for a moment. "OK. I'm in," he said.

Ms. Risk shook his hand. "Welcome to the Danger Patrol," she said.

A drop of rain fell. Then another. And soon Saint Felix was engulfed by a thunderstorm the likes of which it had not seen in years.

Talisman returned to Leiter High, where he switched back to plain old Barton Harper. He had his fingers crossed he could find a way to return home without giving up his secret to his mother just yet. Fortune favored him, because he ran into Nathan almost as soon as he entered the building.

Leiter High had a protocol, that whenever large-scale supers battles occurred, that students could stay on campus until the city had calmed down. Barton had never thought he would be in one of those battles, much less need the policy for cover. But soon Nathan's dad arrived, and he happily drove Barton home, but not before embracing him in a bear hug that nearly drove the air from his lungs.

When he entered his home, he was met by his mother and sister, who also embraced him fiercely. Lucy didn't even snark at him.

Friday dawned nearly thirty degrees cooler than Monday, with a light rain still falling. School was called off due to superheroes for the second time in a week, and Barton slept for a long time.

When he finally woke, he had a shower and breakfast and hung out with his mother and sister. Then he put on a raincoat and headed for Nathan's house. For the second time in a week, they were in the basement, debriefing Barton on his adventures.

"So," Nathan said, "you're gonna keep it up."

Barton nodded.

' "You're sure?" Nathan asked.

Barton nodded.

"People spend their whole lives wondering if they make a difference," Barton said. "Someone once told me that not everyone has to make a mark to live a good life. And I think that's true. But if you have it in you to make the world a better place...to know you made a difference..."

Barton shrugged. "I can't turn away from it," he said.

Nathan nodded his agreement.

"Besides," he said, "I'm pretty sure Ms. Risk is into me."

Made in the USA
Monee, IL
11 June 2022

97612457R00105